chloe

doe

Suzanne Phillips

LITTLE, BROWN AND COMPANY
New York ~ Boston

Little, Brown and Company

Hachette Book Group USA
1271 Avenue of the Americas, New York, NY 10020
Visit our Web site at www.lb-teens.com

First Edition: June 2007

The characters and events portrayed in this book are fictitious. Any similarity to real persons, living or dead, is coincidental and not intended by the author.

Library of Congress Cataloging-in-Publication Data

Phillips, Suzanne.
   Chloe Doe / by Suzanne Phillips. — 1st ed.
      p. cm.
   Summary: As former teen prostitute Chloe Doe reveals her family history to a psychiatrist, the battle of wits she wages with him turns into a life-changing experience for her.
   ISBN-13: 978-0-316-01413-7
   ISBN-10: 0-316-01413-3
   [1. Prostitution — Fiction. 2. Family problems — Fiction.] I. Title.
   PZ7.P54647Chl 2007
   [Fic] — dc22

                            2006025287

10 9 8 7 6 5 4 3 2 1

Q-FF

Printed in the United States of America

Author's Note

For the sake of clarity, I'd like to take a moment to define what may be unfamiliar terms for my readers outside the United States. John/Jane Doe are terms applied to unidentified male/female bodies. Johns are the male clientele of prostitutes. Janes are women without identity, those who are seemingly invisible to the rest of society.

For my readers unfamiliar with the Spanish language, the following definitions may be helpful:

niño/niña—boy/girl
abuelita—grandmother
ramera—prostitute
muchachas—young women
lo siento—I'm sorry
cria—baby
puta—whore
ataúd—coffin

I hope this makes for smoother reading.

this is the place you become miss america

At four p.m. the music plays in rec. This is where we learn a new talent. We will all learn dance or it's back to our rooms for solitude, to think about why we don't want to learn the merengue, to think about why we don't want to hold the sweaty, fat hand of Dolores or Tina, why we don't want to swing across the floor in the arms of one of our own.

They want us to say we were no good but now that's changed and we're ready to go out and work a real job. The nurses, the doctors, our social workers here at Madeline Parker Institute for Girls with Real Problems, they want us to say, Sure, I'll take that job at Burger King. I'll be happy to. And leave our lives on the street behind. No more turning tricks. There's a better life for us. But Burger King doesn't pay the rent, not even on that crackerjack apartment on the Amtrak. It doesn't buy food. It doesn't give us an opportunity.

They think we're out there never seeing tomorrow, but that's all we see: Maybe *mañana* things will be better. Maybe *mañana* I'll win the lottery. Maybe *mañana* I'll meet my one true love.

Things can change that fast.

In the meantime, we paid the rent and ate Hostess cupcakes from the 7-Eleven, and maybe a Slurpee, because it's something we always wanted but were told, No, not today. Which meant not tomorrow. Not Tuesday of next week. Not until you can pay for it yourself. Not unless you know your way around the counter, around the night clerk.

The first question the cops ask you, the first time they pick you up: Where did you live? The time before now. The time when you had parents and maybe brothers and sisters. Where did you live?

How old are you?

Dieciocho.

You're not eighteen. Do you have proof you're eighteen? Show me proof you're eighteen, and this time I let you walk.

What state did you live in? Come on, honey, give me at least that. What state?

California, *mijo.*

You don't sound California. What state?

Do you have a telephone number? From the time before now. Do you know your parents' telephone number?

No *familia. Está no familia.* My family died in a house fire; in an automobile crash; in a boating accident in the Pacific Ocean. Or one after the other to some disease, cancer or AIDS. Or you tell them they moved leaving no forwarding address one day when you were in school. This is the best response. The easiest. No questions asked because you don't have answers. No death certificate, no hospital papers. You say your family vanished.

They call it cultural blending, the way I substitute the *es-pañol* for the English. To emphasize. They say I do it to words that need an extra understanding. And maybe I can get away with it, with my dark hair and almond-shaped, beer-bottle-brown eyes. But my skin is too pale. It's no good. What am I hiding behind the words, the words in Spanish? Why, Chloe, won't you say it in English?

They ask, like I have a secret. Like I'm the Great Houdini slipping out of my former life.

Was it so bad growing up Chloe-white-girl with an education and maybe a good family? Or maybe not a good family. Maybe a very bad family. Is that why? Did your father beat you? Did he touch you like he wasn't supposed to? Did he molest you? Did your father take you into a dark room, maybe your brother's bedroom when he was at school or band practice or sleeping, and anyway, too young to know? Did he take you and take you and take you? And is that why?

I don't live in the streets. Not anymore. Some are disappointed — those who want to know a real ticker. A bomb set to blow any minute.

I have better control than that. I lived in a closet with a toilet and a sink, near the Amtrak. The building roared, the walls pitched with each passing train.

On the street you have to watch out for yourself. I did what I had to to get by. You'd do it, too.

No doors open in this city after eleven p.m. Except car doors, swung open from the inside and a body broken down over the front seat, looking for a little coochie: *Twenty dollars? Thirty dollars? Gets me how much?*

The place they send you when you have the last name Doe isn't bad. Quiet, like the street right after a car backfires, at night, when the sound can travel for miles or hours. The quiet following a sonic boom. Following anger's passage from a closed room. Following a death of any kind.

Quiet that strips the paint from the walls. Here, bird-shit-gray walls peeling like cut hair, curled on unwashed floors and pushed aside from foot traffic.

Madeline Parker Institute for Girls.

Tight-faced Janes, we sit here molting. Yellow, black Janes. Sit in the chair. Sit there. Tell us your sorrows.

They think a little talk will do us good. Confession is the first step to recovery.

They tell us, This is the place that's better than the streets. Better than Manny Marquez and a box with no windows to sleep in. To piss in. To bathe standing at the sink. Ninety-eight dollars a week and you can own this lovely *ataúd*. Be careful it doesn't blow down with the wind. Careful you're not in it when the earthquake comes. Careful it doesn't fall on you like a fate.

This is the place that can change you. Come in. We have a bed for you. We have hot food, as much as you can eat. We have a shower and a window. For you. We have doctors. That rash you have? Gone. The crabs, the herpes? Gone.

This is the place where lobotomies are practiced. Hypnosis: You are no longer a whore, a *puta*. You are a woman. A good girl-woman. When you wake up you will believe this.

Let Dora do your hair for you, a fine braid down your back. Like all the other contestants, in our gray-green gowns. Single file to the dining room, to rec. To group: Talk. Tell us how you're feeling today. Don't be shy. Well, it's OK to be a little. But don't stutter. Points off for stuttering. For touching your hair. For resting your chin in your hand. No points at all for nothing. No TV.

No vote on chocolate cake or canned peaches for dessert. How are you feeling today?

Fine.

Fine?

Better.

Better? Than what?

Cross your legs. Fold your hands like the Mother. This is the place that's better than the streets. This is the place you become Miss America.

jalopy motel

My sister, Camille, and I play Cleopatra and Mark Antony. I'm always Mark Antony, and sometimes a slave-girl, too. Camille is always Cleopatra and only Cleopatra.

She likes the dying scene best.

"Together we built this empire," Camille says, sitting on the front step, on the pillows we took from our beds. "Mark Antony, you are king and I your queen."

"Yes, Cleopatra, Queen of all Egypt."

"But look, Mark Antony, our enemy comes. With thousands more than our own army. We're done." She sighs and her green eyes look like they might cry. "Let's drink our last moment of life, then drink from this cup."

She lifts the silver wine goblet our mother bought for fifty cents at a garage sale. The bottom is uneven and it won't stand. Camille holds it above our heads.

"Together. We must go together. Hold my hand." She reaches out from under her yellow bathrobe and takes my hand. "Drink, Mark Antony. Drink!"

I'm supposed to pretend-sip, then gasp, like something is burning in my throat, then grab at my chest and sink to the ground at her feet, twisting in pain. When Camille pretend-dies she just slips off the pillows and lays herself over my stomach.

Sometimes Camille doesn't drink, but lives on, ordering her slaves to remove my body.

"Take him," she says. "You may throw him in the river." Then she walks away saying, "Stupid, stupid man."

Camille models our mother's favorite nightgown, the one that's put away in her hanky drawer, separate from her others. It's a see-through, gauzy, aqua material with a satin bow in the center, where Camille is developing breasts. Our mother says she wore it on her honeymoon with our father, which was a weekend at the jalopy motel in Borrego Springs, in the middle of the Southern California desert. She has a picture postcard of the motel in the family photo album. There's a swimming pool in front and short bungalows in back. There are palm trees and red lounge chairs and a blue neon sign that reads HONEYMOON HAVEN — NO VACANCY.

Whenever I look at the picture, I see my parents in the pool, laughing and slapping water at each other. I see them sitting on the lounge chairs, holding hands. Our mother says they were happy, at first. That they held hands and had eyes only for each other. I want to fall in love like that one day. I don't say that aloud anymore. When I do, Camille calls me a baby and purses her lips like I'm something bad to look at. I'm in the fifth grade. Next year I'll be moving on to the middle school, and Camille says she won't even notice me if I don't grow up. She'll be in eighth grade and has friends who talk about real love and, she says, holding hands doesn't measure up.

"What do you think of this?"

Camille has changed into our mother's Friday office dress, the one that can be worn out to drinks when she adds a scarf and hoop earrings. Camille stands in front of the long mirror behind our mother's bedroom door. Her feet fit perfectly into our mother's size seven high heels. She turns, pulls on the hem of the skirt, looks over her shoulder for the rear view, turns and watches her profile through a series of smiles and hair adjustments, examines and pokes breasts that aren't really noticeable. I tell her this.

"I have more now than you'll ever have," she says.

"I don't care." But I'm starting to.

"Yes, you do." She's so confident about this, she thinks I'll cry when I'm slow to develop. "Skinny girls are always the last to show on top. You'll have to stuff your bra."

"No, I won't."

Then she picks up the box of tissues from our mother's bureau and begins stuffing them into the front of the office-to-evening dress she's modeling.

"You stuff your bra," I say.

"Of course." And that tone is in her voice, the one that says there's no hope for me.

Our mother met our father in a café off highway 89. Camille thinks it was romantic and our mother agrees. We're sitting at the kitchen table, peeling vegetables, when Camille asks to hear the story again. Our mother stops cutting carrots and looks past us, into her memory.

"I got on the train in Kirksey, Kentucky, and got off in Peeples Valley, Arizona. The first thing I did was go into that café." She stops for a minute, frowning so that the lines spreading out from under her eyes crinkle. "Damn, I wish I could remember the name of that place."

"Millicent's Country Café," Camille says.

"Hell, that's right." Our mother taps the table with her fingers. "I've always said you have a steel trap for a memory.

"Millicent's Country Café. It sounds pretty, doesn't it? I thought at the time it did. I remember standing outside that café and reading that sign and thinking, This is a new beginning. I'm going to start my new life right here.

"I walked inside, sat myself down, and when the waitress came over I asked her what she recommended. Do you know what she said?"

Our mother looks at us for the answer, but we both shake our heads.

"She said, 'I recommend you get back on that train and choose another stop.' That's what she said. She was a wise woman. I wish now I'd listened. Of course, then, I wouldn't have you two darlings." Our mother smiles at us briefly, then props her chin on her hands. "Instead, I ordered a cheese blintz and a cup of coffee and while I was eating in walked your father."

She sits back in her chair; her fingers poke at the ribbons of carrot skins.

"You know, my first look at him I thought I was looking at a movie star. I swear that's exactly what I thought. He was too skinny, of course. But he was tall and handsome, with eyes that looked right at you and made you melt down to your shoes. I think I fell in love with him then and there."

"Did he love you right away, too?" Camille asks.

"Oh, I think so." She shakes the carrot shavings from her fingers. "Maybe not the same minute, but soon after.

"I remember the first thing he said to me: 'That's nice of you to say, ma'am.' I watched him walk into the café and sit down at the breakfast bar. He ordered scrambled eggs and black coffee and his voice was like a song. He had this accent from somewhere far away. I knew it was something European. And I walked up to him and told him how beautiful I thought his voice was."

She gets lost in her thoughts for a moment, until her smile breaks up and she looks at me and Camille with warning in her eyes.

"Your father was very polite. He was a good man to be in love with." She looks at us across the table, her eyes filling with sadness. "If I'd known I'd end up with heartbreak, I might've gotten back on that train."

Camille teaches me to walk in heels only after she can do it gracefully, with the sway of a willow tree caught in the wind.

It took her some time to get to this point. At first her hips moved like water in a bath tub, swooshing from side to side, because her ankles wouldn't stay firm. They turned out, or in, and she lost the shoes trying to right herself.

"I have to exercise them," she said.

She lay on her stomach on the floor, with her feet under the box spring and mattress of her bed, lifting then dropping them, then lifting them again, dropping them. "You need strong ankles."

Now her walk is as sassy as our mother's. And she doesn't want me left behind. Camille says boys don't date girls who wear sneakers with their dresses.

"I don't want a date."

She rolls her eyes. "You will."

Our mother says she's one smart cookie. "It takes more than a body and nice clothes to get your stepfather."

Henrik worked for the government, building fighter planes for our military. When we moved into our new house, our mother told the neighbors, "Henrik is with the government, but we'll keep that our secret." She told everyone who came by to say hello or who brought by something to help with dinner.

Our mother met Henrik right before Christmas last year; they got married on New Year's Eve, with me and Camille standing beside them and a judge in plain clothes and not even a Bible telling us how lucky we were to find each other.

Before that day, I only talked to Henrik once, when I answered the phone. He said the sound of my voice made him miss his own little girl. I asked him if she had a phone, but he took so long answering I hung up.

I'm not feeling so lucky. Neither is Camille.

A month after the wedding our mother went back to her job at the insurance company because that's what she was doing when she met Henrik. And because life would be a bore if she didn't have something to do with herself.

Camille says our mother tried crocheting and took a pottery class, but it didn't fill the holes.

Our mother went back to work for the interaction. She isn't the stay-at-home kind of mother. She needs to have interests. She needs to think about more than what's for dinner and does she have enough chicken. She needs to talk to more than the mailman about additional postage and the grocery clerk about the price of cheese. She needs outside stimulation.

Camille says our mother has to work to help support us because Henrik has his own children from another marriage.

"What's alimony?" I ask.

"It's when you get divorced," Camille says. "It's when the husband pays the wife so she can go on living like she's used to."

Henrik is paying for his wife and children, so our mother was married at the courthouse and they went to Ensenada for their honeymoon. We stayed with a sitter.

"For once I'd like to have a real honeymoon," I heard our mother say. "I don't suppose that will ever happen."

"Ensenada will be nice," Henrik said. "We can lay on the beach."

"Not this time of year," our mother said.

"Sure we can," Henrik crooned. "It's warmer down south."

Camille says Henrik was the best at making our mother happy. "He knew a lot of the right things to say."

The problem was his first wife appreciated it more than our mother did. Three months after Ensenada, Henrik went back to his family.

Our mother blamed it on the honeymoon; Ensenada wasn't much better than Borrego Springs. "Any marriage that starts at the jalopy motel is bound for disaster," our mother says.

walk of stars

"*Tú fea!*" he says, not even looking at me. *You're ugly.*

The little *niño,* playing with his cars and GI Joe, on the floor of my new home. *The Casa de Madeline Parker.*

I tell him, You're breaking my heart, little Romeo.

"*Dolor de corazón.*"

He shrugs his little-boy shoulders, makes the GI Joe crash into a table leg and fall over dead. The car keeps going, without a driver. Not a thought spared for poor GI spread out on his face.

How I got to Madeline Parker:

We agree on a price. He says, "Come on, how 'bout fifty dollars for the whole package? How 'bout it, baby?"

"I'm not your fairy princess," I tell him. "That's half price. What? Is it your birthday?"

"Sixty?" he says.

"You're wasting my time." I move down the sidewalk some, with him crawling after me in his white family sedan.

"Seventy-five? Come on, sweetness, that's all I got."

It's a slow night. I tell him eighty dollars will get him whatever he wants, and we'll take our time.

The Walk of Stars Motel on Sunset is where I do my business. Manny has an arrangement with the clerk. The rooms are old, water-stained, and musty, but I've never been caught up by the police there. Necessity's more important than atmosphere. Most johns aren't thinking about the wallpaper, anyway. They're not saying to themselves, This place needs new carpeting. The maid could've done a better job cleaning.

The beds are king-size, and that's all that matters to any of them:

"Oh, a lot of room here."

"That's a big playground."

I get this guy down to his briefs then say to him, "You want to pay me now? When business is taken care of, I can take care of you."

He says to me, "Sure, baby. Sure, baby. Here's your money."

He hands me four twenty-dollar bills. When I've got them folded in the palm of my hand, already thinking I've made the rent this week, he says to me, "Sorry, honey."

He pulls out a pair of handcuffs and snaps them on my wrists. "I'm the police," he says.

"Where do your parents live?"

"The North Pole. They're Eskimos."

"Yeah? Where do you live?"

I tell him about my luxury apartment, behind the Wal-Mart and next to the tracks.

"You live on McClintock?" he says. "All by yourself?"

"Sí. Por cierto." I wouldn't have it any other way.

"Who pays your rent? You? Your pimp? Who's paying the bills?"

"I pay my own way. I'm independent."

You see, the price of sugar's gone up again. There's no problem making the bills when you're Chloe Doe.

"What are you, fifteen?"

I tell him, Thank you very much. "Nineteen my next birthday."

"Yeah?" Like he doesn't believe me. And he's right. Next year I'll be able to vote, to serve alcohol, to get a job some-place where the men can look but not touch.

"You have any family? Anyone to help?"

It's an extended stay at juvie or Madeline Parker hospital for self-afflicting personalities.

Madeline Parker is better than prison. It's better than the state hospital, where they drug you and tie you to a chair, put you in front of the TV, and turn on *The Price Is Right*. Where you forget what day it is, and even what year.

The decision is out of my hands:

"You want to save this one?"

"You think this one has saving potential?"

Who's to say I deserve this chance more than another girl? Who's to say I'll do more with it?

Sometimes it comes down to a coin toss.

It's luck, good or bad.

It's karma catching up with you.

"Tails it's Madeline Parker."

Have you done one nice thing in your life? Helped someone when they were needing it?

Yes, I've done that much. And more.

The coin falls tails-up.

So I have a little luck this time. I'm worth the taxpayer's money. They put me in a blue van: MADELINE PARKER INSTITUTE. (213) 555-1737.

From the outside it doesn't look like a hospital. It looks like a Spanish hacienda. A spa for the rich and famous. There are red and yellow flowers on the borders and no bars on the windows.

18

"This is your stop," the driver says. "Welcome to Madeline Parker."

He comes around and unlocks my door. "Don't think of running," he says.

He's bigger than a jet and just as quick.

"Where would I go," I say. "All dressed up and no party?"

He says the orange jumpsuit and the plastic cuffs will come off inside.

In the entrance a little *niño* is sitting on his haunches, playing cars. His *abuelita* is walking circles, waiting for visitor's hours, waiting to see her daughter-*puta*. Her *ramera*. Her shame.

"Hello, little *niño. ¿Cómo está?*"

"¡Tú fea!" he says. *You're ugly.*

You're ugly, too. *Cholo.* You'll grow up ugly.

cholos

Our mother says our father was a Romeo. That's why she married him.

"What's a Romeo?" I ask.

"Shut up," Camille says.

"He swept me off my feet. He was a ladies' man, and gallant.

A knight in shining armor." Our mother looks up from her *Vogue* magazine and pins us with her eyes. "If nothing else, remember this about your father: He really knew how to treat a lady. Too bad he had no staying power. Commitment means nothing these days."

Camille and I were not raised on Mother Goose. Our mother read to us her favorite love stories, the ones she discovered in high school and then left home to find for herself. Sometimes she read to us the advice columns from women's magazines. She said my first word was "sweetie." That I began to read at age three, the same year my father left. That I often read to her from the newspaper. I remember she tore out wedding announcements and hung them on the refrigerator; I remember better stories of men leaving their wives and women found lifeless with empty pill bottles clutched in their hands.

"You can have your white knight," she tells us. "Just make sure you stock up on Connoisseurs." A tarnish remover sold on TV. She goes back to her magazine. The sun glares white off the pages. We're in the backyard of our new rented house on Myrtle Street in San Ysidro. Very close to the Mexican border, to Larsen Park and all the yellow and orange umbrellas on Front Street.

Our mother is sitting in a lounge chair under the Pacific palm, drinking Cuervo with lime juice because we're out of fresh limes. She sends us indoors for ice when what she has melts away. Next to her the phone rings and she answers it, sounding breathless, even though all she had to do was lift it from her lap.

Camille listens to our mother's telephone conversations. Our mother talks to her boyfriends in the evenings, while she makes dinner, and on the weekends, when she can find them. She isn't allowed to make personal calls from the office. We're supposed to be outside at this time, even in the dead of winter, when it's raining and the sky gets dark as early as five o'clock. We come in when we get too cold, or if Camille gets bored. Then Camille sits down in the hall near the kitchen and listens. Today, Camille drops the little shovel she's using to pry the weeds loose and sits back on her heels. Her back is to our mother; otherwise she's not even trying to hide the fact that she's listening.

"You know I love you, _____," our mother says. "You know I'd hate it if I never saw you again. It would be the worst thing in the world that could happen to me."

Our mother cries as easily as the women in the movies.

The sun is hotter here than at our other house, the one where we lived with Henrik; our mother needed a new beginning so we moved with only two months left of the school year. It's a big problem for me. Camille is good at making friends; she has one already and another that's a possibility. She says if I didn't read so much I would have more friends, too.

Camille and I are weeding the flower beds for some extra money. We want to buy *Teen People* and mint chocolate chip ice cream at the store later.

We're all wearing sun hats and Coppertone and wraps over our swimsuits. Camille is wearing an old pair of our mother's Polaroid sunglasses. They're prescription and scratched and Camille has to feel the ground to find the weeds.

"I don't want wrinkles," she says. "You get them from looking into the sun."

"What's a Romeo," I ask again, low so our mother doesn't hear.

"It means he brought her flowers and other things. Gifts, you know. Like he was always thinking about her, even when he wasn't with her."

"Oh," I say, and then, my mind made up, "I'd have married him if he wasn't my father."

"He'd be too old for you, stupid," Camille says.

"I mean if he was the same age. If we went to the same school."

"He wouldn't marry *you*," my sister says.

"He wouldn't marry you, either."

"Yes, he would. He liked redheads."

Our mother's a redhead. So was the woman he left us for.

The front yard of our house on Myrtle Street is small. Our mother calls it a matchbox. It has a metal fence around it, waist-high, like the people before us had a dog. My sister says they had a schnauzer; the yard is dug up, like snake holes, and that's what schnauzers do.

All the houses on our block look the same: peeling paint, windows with lace curtains, and lawns burnt brown and yellow from the sun. Everyone is fenced in and BEWARE OF THE DOG signs are posted on every gate, though Camille and I have found only one dog so far, a Doberman that belongs to the Ramirezes, two doors down. Our mother says the signs are for protection.

The boys who go to our school are *cholos*. They're wicked. They follow us home saying,

"Will you touch our pee-pee?"

"We want to see your ta-tas."

"We want to kiss you with our tongues."

They wear blue suit pants from Kmart and skip rocks off the pavement that hit us in the shins and leave knots and purple bruises. Once they hit Camille in the neck and she dropped like in a dead faint. They ran home thinking they killed her:

"Is she dead? Is she dead?"

Camille stays in the road, even though a car is coming. She keeps her eyes closed. She holds her breath.

When it's getting dark they come to our house and lean against the fence, calling our names.

"What do you want?" I ask.

"Your sister OK?"

"She's dead," I tell them. Camille told me to, and I agreed.

"We didn't see no hearse."

"She's in the bedroom," I say. "You want to come in and light a candle?"

One of them starts to cry. I'm ready then to tell them the truth, but Camille is hiding behind the door, digging her sharp nails into my hand.

The next day, Camille pretends to be sick and stays home from school. "This will teach those dirty boys.

"I hate living here," she says.

Men come around looking for our mother. She keeps them

on the porch, but offers them beer. They drink it fast and belch afterward.

They come in pairs. They speak Spanish among themselves, say hello and good evening to me and Camille in English. In the dark, their teeth flash like lightning.

Camille says they're attracted to our mother the way moths are attracted to flame. She says it's because we're *gringas*. Because our skin glows in the dark. Because, underneath it all, we're still American and they're not.

"Hey, *gringas*! Hey, *blancas*!" Laughing men call to us when we walk home from the market with milk and sour whips and our mother's change tinkling in our pockets.

Camille says not to run, but I do anyway. Every time. Their voices sound sweaty and close and getting closer. I run all the way home and wait for Camille by the gate.

She says they're men who have nothing better to do with their time. But they're harmless.

One day I come home from school early because I have a fever and our house is only two blocks away. Our mother was not at work when they called.

We have a working mother. The teachers know that the girls with the white names among the Marisols and Esperanzas and Mercedes can mind themselves. The girls with pancake batter for skin, who wear outlet clothes, they can walk themselves home. Our mother wrote a note saying so. The school nurse finds it in a file and after I dig up my house key and show it to her, she lets me go.

Our mother is in the house with the one Camille and I call Gordo because he's so big. He's sitting on the couch wearing a white T-shirt and nothing else. His stomach rolls out and underneath, his pink worm hangs like a lazy hand.

"*¡Ave María! ¡Jesús, Jesús!*" He grabs his pants off the floor and balls them up in his lap. He calls my mother.

I hear the water shut off in the kitchen.

"Is Chloe, eh?" he says to me.

I nod.

"Chloe! *¡Aquí! ¡Aquí!*" he yells to the kitchen.

My mother is wearing her slippers. I hear them scrape on the floor as she comes down the hall. She's in her bathrobe. Her makeup is worn off.

"I have a fever," I say.

She stands in the entry and looks at me for a long time without saying anything. Gordo stands up and leans over himself as he pulls his pants on.

"You're flushed," my mother says.

Gordo heads for the door and opens it.

"*Adiós.*"

My mother doesn't answer him, and Gordo walks quietly out the door, barely making a noise when he shuts it.

"You want to get in your pajamas?" she asks. "I'll get you some aspirin."

When she comes into my room she says, "I hope it's not the chicken pox."

*   *   *

I tell Camille about finding Gordo naked on our living room sofa, and she says, "That's what you get for playing sick." Even though I really do have the chicken pox.

I'm out of school for two weeks. My mother stays home with me the first day. She feeds me broth and crackers and helps me with my homework. After that, the neighbor checks on me twice a day. Gordo even comes by with flowers for my room, daisies and azaleas from his garden.

My mother thinks the neighbor brought them, but I tell Camille they're from Gordo. Of all our mother's Mexican friends, we like him the best. He smiles more, and we've never seen him drink until he's falling down, like the others.

But Camille says she doesn't want to look at them. She says he's trying to cover up.

"What for?"

"He doesn't want you to tell the police."

"What would I tell the police?"

"It's to keep you quiet," she says.

When I don't say anything back, she says, "You like him, don't you?" Then slams the door shut on her way out.

the joker

There's no desk in here. No couch and no window. The room is so small I begin to feel like I've been shut inside a re- frigerator. Except it's hot, even wearing the tissue-paper top and pants they gave me my first day in. No street clothes, no shoes allowed the first seventy-two hours. We have slippers that pull on like socks. I asked, but so far no girl has made it to freedom tying the slippers together and dangling from her second-story window.

I'm sitting in one of the four chairs in the library. There are few books. The girls have stolen them, ripped the pages, written obscenities where there were none and exaggerated them where there are. Now if we want a book, we have to earn it. They have a list of appropriate behavior and the points you get for each. Saying "please" and "thank you" adds up. At five points a day a girl can get a toothbrush and shampoo by the end of the week. But what does she do before then?

The library is a multipurpose room. Today, there is a hand-written sign on the door that reads: PRIVATE THERAPY, PLEASE KNOCK. Each of us *muchachas* get a shrink from the outside. They come in once a week for one-on-one and every Monday to listen to us talk in a group. There are points for that, too.

I've moved the other chairs into a tight half-circle and have taken the throne for myself. Dr. Queerborn will sit quietly or he'll make a fuss. Maybe he'll say something smart about role reversals. I only know what the others have said about him. Tina and some of the other girls who have sat with him behind closed doors. Who have listened like their lives depended on it. They say he is as wired as a wet cat. That he's tall and skinny and that his dick is probably the same. Some say they would marry him. Tina, who has been here the longest, says what she'll miss the most when she leaves is having someone who nails her without even touching her.

So maybe he's got something, and maybe not.

This is not my first time in a place like this. The state has been trying to change my ways for years. I've been in foster homes, in special schools, in programs they were sure would fix what's wrong with me. Thing is, not one of the places I've been has matched me up with someone smarter than myself. Someone with more common sense than book smarts. Who's lived a little, and not all of it was storybook.

The nurses bring in magazines with the address labels cut out, so that we have to guess who subscribes to *Glamour* and who to *National Geographic*. We don't want their addresses like they think; they're the last people we'll visit when we get out.

I'm reading *Cosmo: The Sex Issue*. Someone underlined the words penis, ejaculation, and burgeoning in an article about male sterility. When the door opens I begin to read aloud, "'Sterility, though it certainly affects a man's sexuality, is a medical disorder . . .'"

I catch glimpses of him as he walks from the door to the chair across from mine and sits down: khaki pants; long, thin hands; and glasses.

"'Bottom line,'" I read, "'the penis ceases to function as desired. This will lead to anxiety. And here, ladies, is where you can help. . . .'"

"How do you like that?" I ask, and look over the top of the magazine. "I'm in the helping profession."

He's smiling. His skin is thin enough I can see through it. So I know he's happy to see me. Or he's happy with himself — he managed to fold up his body and fit it into the space of one chair pulled very close. Our knees almost touch. Either way he's happy and not afraid to show it, and I begin to feel like I'm sitting in a tub of broken glass.

"We have something in common," he says.

His hands are folded in his lap. He looks at me for a long time without blinking.

"I can do that, too," I say. "I won the school staring contest in the fourth grade."

He tells me, "You're not what I expected."

"Maybe you can return me. Exchange me for another *señorita*. We come in a lot of colors."

He shakes his head and waves a manila folder in front of me. "Your file," he says. "You don't look like you've been on the street this long."

I pull my shirt over my head. I'm not wearing a bra — no bra and no belt the first seventy-two hours of my stay, for my protection as well as theirs. I never heard of a girl hanging herself with her bra, or strangling her captors with it, but they say it can be done.

I'm a 36B and as I move my arms, my breasts wave at him. The doctor's face shuts down. It's like a magic wand passed over him. He stops what he was going to say and his ears, the part that light can almost pass through, turn pink. Before he can call for staff, I turn my back and show him the scar. It's a capital C that begins at the top of my shoulder blade and stops at my eleventh vertebrae.

"That was from a knife. I stood on the wrong corner. I was still new then." I put my shirt back on and pull up my pant leg.

"See that? It's a bruise that never goes away." It's faded to brown now but is as big as the day I got it. "From a boot," I tell him. "It's got to be a year old." I straighten my pants and sit back. "You ever been in a fight, Doc?"

"Not since grade school."

"You have any scars?"

He wants to know if surgery counts. The best he can do, he says, is a scar he got when they put a pin in his elbow. He doesn't show it to me and says instead, "We all have scars."

"Maybe you fell walking up the steps of your slum apartment in the *barrio*."

No, he says. He got it skiing. "My elbow clipped a tree. I'm Dr. Dearborn."

He puts a hand in front of me. His fingers are long and square and the nails are clean. "Good hygiene," I tell him. "That's important to a girl in my business."

I make like I'm going to shake his hand but instead I use my index finger to stroke his palm. Goose bumps rise on the back of his hand and he pulls it away, closed now like a clamshell.

He tells me he's sorry he kept me waiting and wants to know, am I comfortable?

"Like you're someone I can tell my secrets to?" I ask him.

"Is it a secret if you're comfortable? Or just if you're not?"

I know how to play this game. The person who answers the fewest questions wins.

I shift in my seat and our knees bump. He's as cool as rain. He doesn't even flinch. "Excuse me," he says, and pushes his chair back two inches.

I tell him I'm penniless.

"I can't pay your bill."

"The city's picking up the tab." He says not to worry. "Why don't we start with how old you are."

Not a question. Phrased to make me feel more like talking. He paid attention in class.

"Eighteen."

"In three or four years?"

"I was born the day Bush became president." The first Bush. He takes a minute to think it out. "Seventeen."

"Congratulations," I say. "Your degree is a real one."

He thinks this is funny. The lines around his eyes and nose deepen. "You're not the first to question it," he says.

I can read his face as easily as a traffic light.

"What do you want to tell me today?" he asks.

Green.

"Who cuts your hair?"

"My wife," he says. "She does a good job of it, don't you think?"

I tell him it's a mistake. "When your job is getting people to trust you, you shouldn't look like The Joker."

He smiles, wide enough that I can count his teeth.

He is quicker than the others who have tried to split me open and look at my insides. Who have diagnosed me as a "product of an abusive home" or "mani[a]cally depressed" or "criminal element."

"Is it my hair or my good mood that disturbs you most?" he wants to know.

"Why don't we get down to business," I say. "What will it take to get out of here?"

I slide off the chair and am kneeling at his feet. I'm so fast, I'm there a full five seconds before he reacts, but then his face rises above me like a red moon. It says STOP without him even having to speak.

"Get back in your seat," he says.

His voice is tight but not angry. His lips are an even line, and I think about why this bothers me. The best I can come up with is that his frown weighs more than his smile.

I stand up so I can look down on him. I'm losing my edge, what keeps me alive on the street. Not caring. Pretending to not care. It's an art and I'm da Vinci. I ease back into my happy-to-be-here face.

"Your hair," I tell him. "It bothers me more than your good mood." In fact, I say, a haircut would dramatically improve our doctor–patient relationship. "After that, we can work on your attitude."

I stole his line and I like my cleverness so much that I smile at him and take my seat.

"OK," he says, "now we have some real work to do. You don't list a living relative."

"I don't have one."

"Your mother's not alive?"

I tell him I doubt it. "Some people die when they lose a loved one." I believe this with my whole body.

"When was the last time you saw her?"

I've lost track of days and mark time now by the hour.

"Guess," he says.

But I don't need to. I remember the exact moment. I could give him month, day, and year. I could tell him the sky was the darkest I'd ever seen it. Even the lights in the homes of the people I knew seemed farther away than the stars.

"When was the last time you saw your mother, Doc?"

"Christmas. She stayed for two weeks."

"A little hard on the wife and kids?"

"Harder on the son. When?"

"You think working out how I feel about my mother will cure me, Doc? You think she's the key to my happiness?"

"You know how you feel about her. You're mad. And that's good. It means you know you deserve better than you got."

I have one of those moments when you know someone's standing on your shadow. He's so fast, I didn't see him coming. I look him in the eye, see he knows it himself. He's got that look athletes get when they win the gold. He's pleased with himself and the whole world.

"I'm not mad," I tell him.

"Yes, you are."

He's so sure of it, my body gets hot and tight. I'm on my way to thinking I want to rip his head off and use it for an ashtray before I realize the psychology he's using on me.

"You're pretty good," I tell him. "But I'm not mad."

Before he lets me go, he tells me what life looks like. "There's the walk into battle. The battle itself. And the walk away." It's a cycle we repeat. Every day. Sometimes it's over small stuff. Sometimes it's life and death.

35

"Our goal is the peace that follows victory. I want you to spend the next week thinking about what that peace would look like to you."

I want to tell him I don't remember winning anything in my life, but my throat is dry and swallowing doesn't help.

"I want you to think about what you have to give up to get it."

the secret to creating you

In each room there are two beds, one long dresser, half to each, and a beveled mirror, the shatterproof kind, so we won't kill ourselves or our neighbor.

They say, No fighting. No taking your *prójimo,* your roommate, your friend and putting her head through the wall, or the door or the window. We will behave like *cuates,* best buddies.

We have our own bathroom, with a toilet and a shower cubicle, a sink and a plastic tree for hanging our toothbrushes. Towels are distributed each morning and checked off a balance sheet when we hand them back: There will be no hanging, no strangulation, no desperate escape attempts out a second-story window.

The bathroom is small. You can't stand inside it and take a deep breath. It's like my old apartment on the Amtrak: a coffin.

The doors to our rooms remain open. There's no exception to this rule. We dress at seven a.m., when we can expect a certain amount of privacy; male staff workers don't check the halls, don't stick their heads through an arch for a Hurry-up, until 7:20.

We eat breakfast at 7:30 and then have an hour of free time, to read the newspaper, watch *Good Morning America,* or talk to staff.

We can make special requests: for a TV show that evening, for some time in the hospital's library, for a hairbrush, for apple juice instead of milk at lunch. They count your points.

Yes, you can watch *Charmed* tonight. Or

No, you've earned only enough for a diary or a turn with the hot rollers. You want that instead?

You want neither. You want your TV show.

Lo siento, they say. Come back when you decide.

Your points are only good for a week, and then you start

over. There's no saving up for something you really want. Like a bar of rose-scented soap.

There's a list of fifteen items you can purchase with a week's worth of earnings:

1. the pick of Friday's rented movie — 18 points
2. use of the unit's Walkman and the new Beyoncé CD — 18 points
3. your choice for weekly chore — 15 points
4. an extra hour before lights out — 15 points
5. an hour of your favorite TV show — 15 points
6. choice of dessert — 15 points
7. writing journal — 12 points
8. hospital library use — 12 points
9. hot rollers — 12 points
10. hairbrush — 12 points
11. toothbrush — 8 points
12. shampoo — 6 points
13. toothpaste — 6 points
14. bar soap — 6 points
15. visitors — 2 points

The morning is for private therapy — there are seventeen girls to be heard and only five days in the workweek. We meet with our self-help groups and our social workers. With visitors from the outside.

The afternoon is lunch, group, chores, and a little free time to think about where we are and where we'd like to be.

We are assigned one day a week to wash our laundry, unless there are emergencies.

We set out plates, cups, and plastic forks and knives for dinner. They don't miss a chance to protect us from ourselves. We, who are unlucky in love, who might use the prongs of a fork to pierce our hearts.

We watch the evening news with Brian Williams.

We bargain for the right to a vegetarian diet when we see it's meat loaf.

More TV.

We thumb through *Cosmopolitan* and *Us* magazine. We sew buttons onto our shirts.

Write letters to friends who have forgotten us.

We talk among ourselves about what we miss the most: the clean, fresh air of our lives on the outside.

We read: *Salem's Lot, The Hanson Brothers: A Biography, The Secret of Creating Your Future, Love's Savage Embrace, Will You Please Be Quiet, Please?*

We count how many days, and has it grown into months, that we've been here.

On Fridays we have occupational therapy: we use the computers to build a résumé; learn how to sit for an interview (legs crossed, hands folded, smile, even if it takes all you've got); we learn how to dress, no flashy colors and nothing above the knee on show; they teach us a proper handshake; we role-play the perfect scenario.

Business leaders from the community come and tell us what they like to see in an applicant: nicely groomed, smile, know your stuff, be polite. They'll be trusting us with their livelihood — their customers. We'll be the front people, representing the business. We can't chase away their only source of income.

On Tuesdays and Thursdays we have recreational therapy. Physical exercise is important for a full recovery. The endorphins are a natural high. You can't be unhappy when you're running three miles around the gym floor. You'll feel better physically and you'll feel better about yourself. You'll like who you are. Exercise is the key to changing your future. It's control.

We play basketball and learn the importance of a team spirit. Of cooperation. People depend on you. You don't want to let them down.

Do something wrong and you lose. You've let down your team. You feel shame, if you're any kind of team player.

This kind of lesson works in your everyday life, they say. Teamwork will help you get along with others. You'll love your neighbor. You'll stop at the scene of a car accident and give first aid. You'll develop a world conscience — you'll want to recycle, you'll stop using plastic, and you'll shut off the light when you leave a room.

On Wednesdays we have art therapy. The first week we made greeting cards. They went to all the *carrozas* in the nursing home down the street. We learn to crochet or knit. We sew holiday crafts: wreaths that went to the local churches and ornaments that went to hospitals. We paint with watercolors. We mold clay into ashtrays or hot plates. Some of our things are sold at the hospital auxiliary.

They tell us we do the art to vent our frustrations. To provide a welcome hello to forgotten people. To let someone who's suffering know there's someone who knows. We do it as an outlet for bottled pain and violations.

Lights-out is ten p.m. We lay in our beds and wish we could fall asleep without remembering other times we lay in bed and wished we could just fall asleep. Or play dead. In our homes, where we had maybe a mother who was blind and deaf and a father who stole our secrets.

made in america

Today is my first time in group and all the other *chicas* with their long nails tap-tap-tapping against the arms of their chairs are waiting for my story.

"I'm one of the best," I say. I can nickel-and-dime them down to the lint in their pockets.

"That's why I do what I do, Doc. I'm a natural." I was born into my trade.

"I have *talento*."

A real gift.

You get them really hot. You get them so all they're thinking about is getting off, they're begging for it, *Baby, baby, now!* And I say, That's going to cost you a little more. We've already run through the sixty-dollar happy hour.

By then they're willing to pay.

That's one of the benefits of the job. Any extra is yours. Manny Marquez never knows. And what he doesn't know is good for me.

Dr. Dear leans forward in his chair. "Tell us more," he says. Tell us a typical day in the life of Chloestreetwalker, he says. "What is it like? What concerns you the most?"

Today he's playing dress-up in a white coat like the other doctors. I like him better when he shows a little of himself. When he looks less like he's practicing and I'm the mouse in the spin wheel.

Here it is, I say, my autobiography.

There are some troubles in my line of work. Sure. Things that make you wonder if you're ever going to get ahead.

AIDS. You worry about that all the time. Even while you're suiting up. Even when you have him all wrapped up in a gold-seal Trojan, you worry if this is the one that's got the hole. Is this the one that's going to break? Is he poison? Is this one seventy-five-dollar trick going to have it in for me?

Then I say to myself, Can't be. That's not the way I'm going. I had a premonition: death by drowning.

I dream about it. I feel it inside like it's happened to me before. In another life maybe. Or did I drown when I was a baby, was saved, and remember only the feeling of it? Like suffocating. Tumbling, and then the sweet oblivion. Not caring if I get a last breath. I've found what I've been looking for all my life.

So I figure it's got to be drowning. Or maybe strangulation. Maybe some twisted john's going to get me with an extension cord. But he's not going to kill me off slow.

My death is decided and AIDS doesn't come into it. But it's something that's always at the back of my mind. It's got to be. It keeps me careful. It's enough of a worry that any john that looks sick, any beyond skinny, any with scabs on his face or hands, and I say, No, thank you. I tell him, unless he has a bona fide, signed and sealed certificate of health dated yesterday, I don't do it.

"Not for a hundred dollars?"

Not for a thousand. Not for ten thousand dollars and your Cadillac. I've still got things to do with my life.

Another thing is junkies. They're so hooked on smack, they'll break your hundred-dollar trick by doing it for twenty.

It's robbery. They undermine the business. You get ten crackheads out on the street on a good night and your take is half what it should be.

We try to run them out. But they come back, sure as roaches. The streets are infested with them.

They bring down our worth. When it's, I'll die for a hit, a smack, a shot of the stuff, you can forget asking seventy-five dollars for what a coke whore will do for pennies.

They're killing themselves, and us, too. If I had one wish I'd wish they'd get the job done. If they're going to kill themselves, then do it. We have rent due. We have to eat.

How do you know you have a lunatic on your hands? It's in their eyes. If he looks at you too long and there's nothing going on inside his head, you have a potential problem. Now, most johns, they get excited looking at you. They breathe heavy. Their eyes glaze over. Maybe they're panting. Any of this, it shows in their eyes.

I've seen it a couple of times when the eyes lay as flat as the desert. One time I went along with it, even though I was thinking I shouldn't. Even though warning bells were going off inside my head.

I needed the cash. It was that simple. We had a week or two of rain and the rent was due. I went against my better judgment.

It turns out this guy needed more than twenty minutes of my best work and still there was nothing to show for it. First he's embarrassed, then mad. He starts yelling that I'm no good, that he wants his money back.

In a circumstance like this, the last thing you do is complain. Instead, you back off easy. I said, I guess I'm just not your lucky number tonight. I guess I lost my golden touch.

I told him, "I had the same problem just the other night. I guess it's time I found myself another career."

And maybe laugh about it, like it's nothing.

Then you get out of there. Quick.

That's how I handled it. The other times I had a psycho asking me for it, I walked away. No thank you, polite as can be. And kept walking.

Any job has one or two things about it you don't like. You put up with it because it comes as a package deal.

That's how I look at the cops. As a minor inconvenience. They come, they get you to offer them a good thing, they arrest you. You're in juvie a month or two, in foster care for less, then back to square one.

The finances are messed up. All for him and none for you. It seems like I get my rent paid, buy groceries, stockings, a pair of working shoes, and there's nothing left. Meanwhile, Manny's got a cream car and silk shirts. These things don't get by me.

Most of the time I think, Well, look at him, he's got fifteen girls he's running interference for. That's a big job. At least he doesn't hit me. He isn't some masochistic SOB, and I should be grateful for that. But one day I'm getting out. Moving on to something better.

I'm going to get on a service. I've got the looks for it. I've got the business sense. I knew some girls who made it into the big time. Made top dollar, and kept half of everything they pulled in. I knew a girl who had a credit card machine in her apartment. Visa, Mastercard, American Express. She took it all. And the work, cream of the crop.

So it wasn't all bad. There was room for advancement, if you had what it took to get ahead.

That's what I was looking for. A way to the top. I kept my eyes open, too. I wasn't out there thinking of the moment and nothing more. I thought about my future.

I thought of myself as a commodity. American made. I thought, Somebody will come by who can't resist the packaging.

And then it was *¡Adiós! ¡Hasta la vista!*

That's the way it works. Someone likes what he sees, and BAM! You're outta there.

It was like treading water, waiting for that to happen. It was like any job, with things you didn't like about it, and fringe benefits that made it worth sticking around for a while.

This is my song. I made it up myself. They let me in the library, the nurses who liked my attitude, me wanting to get ready for my moment in the sun, my first group and having something to say for myself.

My song says it all, my little rap better than anything Latifah comes up with. This is how I was, when I was on the street:

I'm the American Dream.
I'm your inspiration.
Your destination.

I'm a woman of independent means.
I have it all:
Liberty; *libertad; liberación.*
I'm the American flag.

I'm a franchise.
A lawless indiscretion.
Outspoken, downright shameless;
I'm loose.

I'm redemption.
The key to your happiness.
I'll see you through to tomorrow.
Today. *Hoy.*

I can make you as good as new.
Instantly.
Before you can say Jack Robinson.

I am the cure.
The serum.
One shot of me and you're hooked,
Line and sinker.

I'm an addiction.
A craving.
I'm nicotine and kerosene.

You'll burn for me.
Chain-smoke me.
Toke me.
Intravenously stroke me.

I'm tradition,
Like marriage vows and first sons.
I'm your inclination.
And destination.

It's not cosmic.
There's no rocket's red glare.
No love at first sight.
I'm no wonder of the world.
I'm the American Dream.
I'm small business at its best.
I'm success in the flesh.

You see, Doc? It's a matter of natural selection. Birthright.
Darwin knew what he was talking about.

live birth

A girl I knew used a wire coat hanger. Clinics only take you after you prove you're old enough to make the decision yourself. They don't care if you don't have parents. That you've been living on your own a long time. The law is the law.

She said the ladies at the clinic gave her a five-page

questionnaire and had her sit for an hour in a plastic chair, waiting her turn for review. Then they tell her, Sorry. Sorry. You have to prove you're old enough. It's the state law. Have you told your parents?

She asked them, "Is there a state that doesn't have this law? Is there a place I can go?"

It turns out she can go to Mexico or the state of Maine. Either is a world away.

She waited. She said the pregnancy began to fester. Johns don't like you if you're *embarazada*. She began to show. She couldn't buy food. She was behind on her rent. When johns don't take you there's no way to pay the bills, unless you steal. She tried taking a can of soup and Doritos from a family market on Haines Street, but they ran after her. She threw it back at them and kept running so she wouldn't go to jail.

She said she thought of throwing herself in front of a car. But that would mean the welfare hospital. Beds are filled and you're put on a cot in the hall, with people bumping into you, their talking and crying keeping you up all hours, and them butting into your personal business: "What happened to you? You look horrible, a mess. What happened to you?" There's no privacy.

She thought she could use the hanger and do enough damage that the baby would come unglued and come out of her like a blood clot.

She said it felt like electricity moving around inside her. And then she began to bleed.

She bled like it was raining. Like it would never stop.

She told me she stumbled into the emergency room, the clean one at Cedar's where the stars go, and they had to take her. She was a true emergency.

They took her baby from her like it was a live birth.

She said the wire coat hanger was the best choice open to her. She said she would have to do the same again if it came to that.

She was in the hospital four days, and when she left they gave her a three-month prescription of birth control pills and a dozen condoms and told her to go to the county clinic when she ran out.

This girl, she said it was nothing. Not at all like the horror stories you hear where the girl dies, all bloody and crying for her *mamá*. She didn't think of her mother at all during her crisis. It was a few minutes of pain and wondering if she was going to die. She thought about her place. Who would come and go through her things? Would they keep the good stuff? Or would they think it was junk and throw it all away? That's the kind of thing that went through her mind.

She said the bleeding told her enough to go to a hospital, but she waited twenty minutes just to make sure the baby couldn't be saved. She didn't want to go through all that and still have a pregnancy, another mouth to feed when she couldn't feed her own.

Then she went outside and got herself a cab and said, Cedar's Sinai, like she was somebody. Like she was a movie star. And they took her. They had to. She was likely to bleed to death.

"If you can have an at-home birth," she said, "there's no reason you can't have an at-home abortion."

She did it just fine.

"I'm a pioneer in birth control methods. They'll write a book about me. Write me into *historia*."

little *niña*

I have a roommate. Her name is Mary Christine. She is not like the rest of us, who have done it for a place to live, for groceries, for makeup and a pair of tall boots. Mary Christine slept with her brother.

"He's in prison now," she says. But not for the sex, which started when Mary Christine was nine and her brother thirteen; when her brother changed his name to Jesus and convinced the little Niña they were saving the world. Mary Christine's brother killed their father. "He'll be there for a long time."

Mary Christine's real name is Tammy. In group, at lunch, passing in the hallways, we have to call her Tammy, but alone in our room she asks me to call her Mary Christine; she still believes everything her brother told her. I pretend I'm Switzerland and make up my own name for her. She is young, fourteen, and too innocent for us. Still a girl, really.

The little Niña is the only one of us with a regular visitor who isn't our social worker or shrink. Her mother visits every Tuesday. She arrives at exactly nine a.m. and stays until they ask her to leave.

She walks into our room like she's returning from the market: "Mom's here!"

The little Niña, sitting on her bed, turns a page in her magazine. She pulls her knees up to her chest and hums. Not a song, but the buzz of a housefly, of a jet engine.

"Now is that any way to say hello to your mom?" Mrs. Jacobs swats the Niña's leg with a leather glove. She wears them driving. She has a toy dog, too. She sometimes brings him, shut up in her purse. "I brought you something special today," she tells the Niña. "And don't let them take it away from you this time." Her white, white hand is stuffed in her purse, hunting.

Staff doesn't throw away the things her mother brings; the little Niña does it. She tears them up, even if it's a pillow or a favorite shirt, and flushes the pieces down the toilet.

"I can't believe I found this," her mother says. "It was inside a book, on the desk in your bedroom."

The special something is a baby picture of Mary Christine, only the photo has been cut. In it Mary Christine is wearing a blue, fluffy dress, her hair is lighter, almost blond, and curly. In front of her folded legs is a third foot, larger, laced into a brown boot. Mrs. Jacobs lets the photo slip from her fingers onto the magazine and into Mary Christine's lap.

Mary Christine picks up the photo and brings it close to her face.

"Where is he?" the Niña shrieks. "What did you do to him?"

"Who?" Mrs. Jacobs asks. She has forgotten her only son. Shut him out of her heart when she woke from the gunshot blast and found herself soaked in her husband's blood. "What are you talking about?"

"My brother."

"You don't have a brother, Tammy," Mrs. Jacobs says, her face as closed as a door. "It's just me and you."

"No. No. No." Mary Christine holds the photograph against her face and cries.

Mrs. Jacobs picks up her purse. She slips her hands into her gloves. "I don't know what I'll bring next week," she says. She's slowly moving Mary Christine's belongings out of their tidy home in the Hollywood Hills. "How about your yearbook? You don't want to forget your friends."

Later, the Niña tells me she feels like a dirty dish towel her mother twists, twists, wringing out the only part of her that matters.

She won't tell me her brother's real name. Mary Christine writes *Hey-Zeus* letters staff won't mail. Instead, the Niña tucks them into her diary, where no one, not even staff, is allowed to go. She writes him a letter telling him they don't want her to have the baby. The doctors are saying the baby will be retarded. He won't be able to talk. He'll spend his life in bed, crying or unconscious. He won't know she is his mother.

"I think all babies know their mother," she tells me. She looks at me over the letter in her hand. "Don't you?"

"Depends," I say. Having a baby at fourteen is plain *loco*.

She's in her third month and will have to decide. Before, the pregnancies ended on their own. One when Mary Christine fell out her bedroom window, which is on the second floor. The other naturally.

Her pants are tight. She doesn't button them, but they're difficult even to zip. The nurses bring her clothes from their homes that will make her more comfortable; her mother won't accept that Mary Christine is having her grandchild.

Mrs. Jacobs tells Tammy on her next visit, when she comes in the middle of the day, with a long envelope and a bag of the Niña's clothes, that she must choose to abort. She shows her pictures of babies born in-family. Some have their noses smashed into their faces, others are missing ears and toes. They never say mama. They never look into your eyes and say I love you. Some of them don't even have eyes. Some of them are so messed up, an arm comes out of a leg socket. Does she want a baby like that, her mother asks. One that will suffer every day of his life?

Mary Christine doesn't answer. She clutches the bag of clothing, pulling out pieces — a pair of jeans, underwear, a cheerleading skirt — until it's all piled in her lap.

Her mother leaves the pictures spread out on the bottom of the Niña's bed and walks out.

Mary Christine doesn't choose to keep or do away with the baby. It's by God's intervention that her third baby is taken from her. This is what she says. She is in group one week after her mother came with the pictures. Her stomach is gone, flat as pavement. Her face is as angular and as starved as the face of the real Jesus.

"The baby is gone," she says. She doesn't cry. She's holding a small crocheted beanie she made during rec time.

"Gone where?" the doctor asks.

The Niña shrugs. "Heaven, I suppose."

I think about this. Do all babies go to heaven, even those who never take a breath?

crank

Speed, crank, meth, crystal, ice.

Swallowed, smoked, snorted, injected.

A cheap high. An epidemic.

In group they ask us to talk about any and all drugs we've used and why we think we'll go back to it when we get out.

"I never used. Not the hard stuff."

My blood hasn't been tainted. I never feel the need crawling on my skin, digging into me like claws or fangs.

Really?

They don't believe me.

I know a lot about drugs. Mostly what they do to a person, and I picked that up watching my *cuates*. A person uses them enough, they're wasted on or off of them.

Hitler used speed. He was an *aficionado*. Passionately devoted to the stuff. They don't tell you that in the history books. Stick with me, Chloe Doe. I'll let you in on all the dope.

Your parents pop little white pills for a long-haul vacay. Drive through the night, and the next, and you asleep in the backseat, headlights passing overhead. Before you know it you're at Grandma's.

It's not new. For a while coke was the drug of choice, but for the working class, it got expensive. Zap! Back into the limelight.

Twenty-five dollars of coke gets you an hour high. Twenty-five dollars of meth gets you three, sometimes five hours.

You can't beat that. More for your money.

And it's the same thing. Gives you the same rush. You feel like you can run a marathon and discover the cure for cancer.

I've seen labs set up in motel rooms. In garden sheds. In mobile homes way out in the middle of nowhere, that suddenly become the center of activity. First giveaway. That's when you're too doped up to be making it. There's a general street rule: if you're making it, you shouldn't be taking it.

Last year a lab blew the roof off a house in East L.A. and set the whole block on fire. It exploded like it was the Fourth of July. I never saw anything like it. Houses went down like cardboard, and all the firemen scrambling like busy little bees, and dumbstruck. What can you do? It was a meth lab.

The little niña-woman, my roommate, confesses: She swallowed a bottle of baby aspirin. She was nine. Her parents rushed her to the hospital and they pumped out her stomach. She said she ate Mexican for dinner and it came up like acid. It burned her nose. Small chunks of tortilla chips got stuck in her throat. It made her cry.

Her parents stood next to the bed wondering if she was going to die. Her mother said, "Save my baby. Please, please, please." And the father rubbed the mother's arms and told her there was no chance Tammy was going to die. It was just a bottle of baby aspirin, for God's sake. Just a bottle of baby aspirin.

This *inocente,* she said she thought at the time, listening to her father talk about the baby aspirin as if it was a moron's choice of relief, that she should have taken the Tylenol. It was on the top shelf of the medicine cabinet and if she'd been more into it, if she'd thought it through rather than thinking anything would do, she'd have grabbed a bottle of something that would work.

Hospitals don't take childhood suicide attempts for real. They asked her, Why did you swallow the baby aspirin? and she told them she did it because she liked the way they tasted —

like vitamin C and a little bit like Tang. They're also a pretty color, like orange SweeTarts.

Turns out the little Niña has a habit, all right, but it's not drugs. She didn't fall out her window — she jumped. She didn't break a bone in her body. Didn't come close to killing herself. It was a call for help, the doctors say. First the baby aspirin and then the window.

She asked for help the only way she knew.

"But there are better ways of getting a person's attention," they tell the Niña. "Better ways of asking for help." Tammy doesn't need to hurt herself to get it.

"Tammy didn't turn to drugs to soften the edges of her reality," the doctors say. She was stronger than that.

Before they turn on me they tell the Niña she's to come up with two things she could say to the right people when she needs help. They don't tell her who the right people are, only that she has until next group.

"Chloe? What do you have to share?"

I don't have a story like the Niña's to tell. I don't even have a story about drugs. Not the hard stuff. Not the stuff that can really mess you up.

"Like I told you before, I've only smoked marijuana." And I only used it as an aphrodisiac — to get my appetite up. Marijuana heightens the senses. The food tastes better and you want more of it.

It's a love potion. The sex, you don't mind it. It gets so you're not really a part of it.

"How long were you a marijuana user?"

They want to know. Here, let me check my calendar. Looks like I started May 15, 2002, at two p.m. How about that? I'm some record keeper. Think that's a marketable skill?

"How long, Chloe?"

It's not a big deal. I tell them soon they'll legalize it. It has medicinal purposes. And it looks like I had a head start. Looks like I'm a pioneer. I knew all about its potential even before the doctors. How about that?

"But how long?"

If I smoked cigarettes it'd be no big deal, right? I mean, cigarettes kill you. It's a known fact. Check your *New England Journal of Medicine* for that. It's in the newspaper. It's on TV. It's on posters at bus stops.

Marijuana's a gift. It's like eyesight to the blind.

Farmers are starting to grow it.

How long? How long? Their faces stretch and thin out like Silly Putty: How long, Chloe? Their voices, too. Deep and winnowed. How long?

"Chloe, here's your pamphlet. Read it and be ready to talk next drug dependency group."

And no points today. No shampoo or toothpaste.

The brochure says: Marijuana: a habit-forming drug obtained from the dried leaves and flowers of the Indian hemp, used as a hallucinogen.

I never saw things. I never smoked and a whole other world sprung up in front of my eyes. Furniture never moved. The *cucarachas* never danced.

I've never *had* to have it.

You crave it, sure. Because it's an escape. But it's not something that gets under your skin.

How much? Was it every day? Or just a Saturday night kind of thing?

"Four years, give or take," I tell them. "And not always. There were long months when I went without it.

"Marijuana's like aspirin. Except you can't OD on it.

"You take it for the little aches and pains.

"Only when I needed to. When I wanted to get away from it all for a few hours. Like a Caribbean vacation, only low budget."

the all-knowing

Camille thinks God can't watch all of us at the same time. "He only has two eyes," she says. "He sends angels to do it."

We're sitting on the blankets from our beds, in our new swimsuits. Camille is already pink, even though she rubs on sunblock 30 every five minutes and it's only May.

"That's what it means to have a guardian angel," she explains.

She thinks her angel is a man in a brown suit who smokes cigars and carries a notebook crammed full of her good deeds. She dreamed it more than once, and Camille believes dreams are as important as our waking moments.

"They're a window into our future."

I tell her, "I dreamed I could sing all the songs on *Breathe*."

"You can do that now, Mom listens to it every day. I dreamed I went somewhere in an airplane. There was snow. Lots of it, on the ground and in the air. And the people spoke a different language, but I understood it. I think I'm going to live there. When I'm eighteen."

"Well, maybe I'll have the same dream," I say.

"You won't. It doesn't happen, two people dreaming the same thing. But you can visit."

"Maybe," I say. I'm done telling her how I want us to be together all the time, even after we're grown. Camille says families aren't meant to be together forever. "We all grow up and go our own ways and meet up again at Christmas. Or," she says, "we catch up on the phone."

Our mother has only two aunts living, she thinks, somewhere in Georgia, and she doesn't keep in touch with them because they're too old to remember her. They don't know that she was ever married or that she has two kids.

"I don't know," I say. "Maybe I'll move somewhere, too. A place where I can ride horses. You can come visit me."

"Okay," she says. She picks a dandelion off its stem and holds it under her chin. She wants the sun to do its magic, to turn her skin yellow without her even touching the weed to her throat. "You're supposed to do it with buttercups," she says, "but we don't have any. Does it make my skin yellow?"

I look under her chin. "Yes."

"Good. That means I'm a ray of sunshine." She drops the weed on the ground.

"What about the things we shouldn't have done?" I ask.

"What things?"

"Does your angel keep track of the things you shouldn't have done?"

She looks at me for a long minute, quiet, the way our mother sometimes does, then says, "Angels can only see the good in people."

But I think God knows everything we do.

Camille has things to hide, like letting Isaiah Riordan kiss her under the flaminca bush in our backyard, lighting matches and burning Simon's ear, and her first period.

She was up in the middle of the night, moving in the darkness. I heard the dresser scrape against the carpet when she pulled it away from the wall, and the lamp fall over.

"What are you doing?"

"Shut up."

"You broke the lamp."

"The lamp isn't broken. Now shut up."

It's a Best of Disney lamp, with Mickey Mouse and all his friends falling out of a tree house, left in the house by the people who rented it before us. I found it first and it's mine. Besides,

Camille's talking like she has a secret, low and choked, like she does when she's in trouble and worried about it.

I turn on the lamp.

"Mind your own business, Baby-Know-It-All."

Camille climbs back into bed and curls up on her side. Her small hands clutch the sheet.

"What are you hiding?" I stand up and look behind the dresser. "What is it?"

"Your bloody underpants."

I stare at her.

"Idiots stare," Camille says. "Bennie Munger."

Bennie Munger is the retarded boy who lives down the street.

Soon my mouth will hang open, and I'll spit when I talk. "You will," Camille says. "Just like Bennie Munger.

"I'm doing you a favor," she says, but she's crying. Not the whole-body sobs I cry, but the pretty, quiet tears. "We wouldn't want Mom to know, would we?" she says. "We wouldn't want her to find them."

"They're not mine."

"Yes, they are. You're a woman now, Chloe. You're all grown up."

"No, I'm not."

"Yes, you are. You can't hide from it. There's no escaping it. It finds you no matter what."

"Liar!"

"It's true. Our Chloe is a woman. Welcome to the club." Camille sniffs and wipes under her nose with the edge of the sheet.

"You're a liar," I say.

"We'll see."

"I'm telling Mom. Then we'll see. We'll see who's all grown up."

"Mom will yell."

"At you. They're your underpants."

She jumps onto my bed and pins me to the mattress with her arm on my throat.

"Never tell, never tell, never tell." She chants our voodoo. I feel a tear drop on my face and run into my ear.

"They're your underpants," I say, but my voice is weak and I can feel the fight drain out of me. I want to know. I'm ready to admit to anything so long as Camille'll tell me about her body's change. Our mother warned us about this event just weeks ago:

"You two are growing up," she said, turning away from the sink, where she was washing the dinner dishes. "No doubt about that." She shook her head, then looked down at me and Camille, still sitting at the table. "You know that, I bet. Jesus, Camille's got boobs." Our mother laughed a little and Camille frowned and started saying how she didn't like the word boobs, and could we please call them something else, when our mother said, "Yes, OK, breasts. Camille, you're growing real fast. I think I was fourteen before I had anything to show for it.

"And you're almost eleven now, Chloe-girl. You want to show us what you got? See if maybe it's time for a bra?" I shook my head and felt my cheeks heat up. Our mother reached down and stretched the T-shirt I was wearing tight across my chest. "Almost," she said. "A couple more months." She let go of my shirt and reached for her cigarettes. She lit one and blew the smoke out in a long cloud over our heads. "Hmm," she said, eyeing me and Camille through the smoke. "You got your period yet, Cammy?"

Camille hates her nickname, but our mother insists on it half the time. She also hates talking about her boobs, unless it's to flaunt them at me.

Camille sank lower in her chair. I heard her feet tap on the linoleum floor, once, twice, three times. "No, I'm not that grown yet."

Our mother thought about this, tilting her head to one side and considering Camille from that angle. She took another drag off her cigarette and flicked the ash into the sink. "You'd tell me though, wouldn't you, girl?" She blew smoke rings at Camille. "Wouldn't you, hon?"

Camille didn't say anything. She kept looking at the tabletop, turning her fork in circles.

"Of course, you'd have to. I mean, you'll need some things." She put her cigarette down on the edge of the sink and walked over to us. "It's just that I started mine by this time. I'm just wondering is all, Cammy."

"I won't tell you if you keep calling me that. If you wanted my name to be Cammy, why didn't you just put it like that on the birth certificate?"

"It's just a nickname, girl." Our mother leaned toward us, putting her skinny hands palms down on the table. "You're a little sensitive lately, Camille. I think that change is coming on pretty soon."

Now, Camille looks at me for a long time, like she's considering her next move. Then she shrugs her shoulders and takes her arm off my throat.

"So what?" she says. "It'll be you soon, too."

She rolls over and lies next to me.

"Why are you crying?"

"I don't know. I guess it's something you do at a time like this."

"Are you sad?"

"No, not really. It's more like a feeling of aloneness. Like no one else knows what's going on inside me. It's a little scary, too. And a relief it's finally come. It's a whole bunch of things. But it's not bad. Not as bad as they tell you in school."

"Are you going to be sick?"

"No. Crampy, maybe. I don't know yet. So far I feel OK. There's a girl in my P.E. class who says she gets cramps every time."

I hope this doesn't happen to Camille.

"I won't tell. Not Mom or anyone."

"Ever?"

"Not ever."

Camille doesn't want our mother to know because she'll drag Camille to the store for the "necessary supplies," and Camille says she can see it already, standing in line at the Safeway and our mother saying to the checker, "My daughter just started. Isn't that amazing? I swear she was in diapers just two months ago." I think I'd keep it to myself, too.

For now, Camille says her P.E. teacher gave each girl a package of necessaries and it will get her through.

"Can I see it?" I ask.

"No."

Camille goes back to her bed but keeps the light on.

"I'm going to sleep with it on. If that bothers you, too bad."

But it doesn't bother me. I know I won't sleep now anyway.

Our first week in our house on Myrtle Street, Camille ran away for an afternoon. She packed her suitcase and left the house like she was going to school, then sat down at the train station and watched the trains and the people until it got dark.

Camille says the train station is full of possibilities.

"There's one train that goes to San Francisco and another one that goes to Santa Fe. You can go to Seattle or Denver or Chicago. One day I'm just going to hop on one of those trains and see where I end up."

"You can try that," our mother says. "But I wouldn't recommend it." She looks up from her nails. She's painting them Scarlet Fever in preparation for her date tonight. She's going out with a man whose truck got hit from behind at a red light. Our mother filed the claim for him and took a picture of the damage. "I tried it once," she said. "Remember?"

That's how she met our father.

"Think about that, Camille, when you're thinking about where that train might take you. My life hasn't been the same since."

I look at Camille. She's got her lips pulled in like she does when she thinks hard about something. I wonder if sometimes our mother thinks about leaving us like our father did. I used to ask her, but she always said, "Don't go borrowing worry, Chloe,"

or "You worry something too much and it's likely to happen," so I
stopped asking.

"I think it might be worth the trip," Camille says.

The next day Camille wrote the school a letter saying she was
at the dentist and would they please excuse her absence. She
signed our mother's name to it.

I haven't told on Camille, not on any of these things. She
didn't need to use her voodoo on me.

I keep my mouth shut because telling means I'm no longer
useful. Sometimes Camille says to me, Get lost. I don't need you.
When I know something, when the secret's still safe, she likes me
better than she likes her best friend.

Camille says she and I will never truly be friends because
she'll always be older, and because of that, smarter.

"We'll never be equals," she says.

At thirteen she's got a mind of her own. I heard our mother say
that about her.

Camille says, "You'll always be running to catch up to me."

When I mention God knowing everything we do to my
mother, she says, "That's some imagination, Chloe-girl. That's
really something. What a thing to turn on your mother."

Then she thinks about it and says, "You know, I think you're
right. Something that off the wall's got to be true. I guess I better
think twice before I eat those grapes in the supermarket. Money
first, then nibble. Huh, Chloe? You think I should think twice?"

Her laugh gets caught in her throat. "You think God knows where your father is? I'd love back pay."

She wears her black dress with the silver bows at the waist and leaves us with a bowl of popcorn and Pepsi and the TV until the houses and the street are quiet, then she comes home, falling on the steps and laughing and saying, "Shh . . . my girls . . ." And there's a man's voice, crashing like thunder, laughing with her.

They make kissing-smacking sounds while Camille and I scrunch down under our covers. And in the morning his car is still in the driveway.

This, I think, is one of the things God knows about that our mother wishes He didn't. In the morning, our mother shows the man to the door then comes into the kitchen bundled in her bathrobe and white in the face, even with her makeup still on. She sits down at the table and says, "Get me a cup of coffee, will you, Camille?" Then she looks at me, in that quiet way of hers. Her eyes get small and the lines under them deepen. "How about that, Chloe?" she says. "You think your mother might have a screw loose?" She tries to light a cigarette but her hands shake and she drops the match. "I think I might. Yeah. That would explain some of the things I do.

"I hope God's given the two of you a little more sense than He gave me."

She looks at Camille, sipping her orange juice. "I worry about you, girlie-girl. A train won't take you where you want to go."

faith

Our second one-to-one, he's waiting for me. The chairs are arranged so that two face each other, with enough room between them an elephant could pass through and fart and we wouldn't hear it. I sit down, in my hospital greens, and really look at him. It's possible he could change my life. I haven't forgotten the way he jumped under my skin, pushed at my soft spots so that I left feeling like a car wreck. No one's ever done that before, gone after me fast and furious and got a hit.

Part of me wants to run, but even I know I wouldn't get far.

He tells me I'm looking better.

My cheeks have filled out some and I've graduated from tissue paper to cotton the color of puke.

"You brushed your hair," I say. I liked it better when it flew away from his head like a scream.

In the week since I've seen him I forgot a lot of details, including the fact that he wears glasses and has a nose a bird could build a nest on. But the hair, I remembered.

"So did you."

"Yeah. They let me have a brush today. A loaner." They don't know about lice here. How easy it is to give each other bugs and infections.

By next week, he says, I could have enough points to buy my own.

"Maybe."

I don't like the point system, that someone else decides the worth of every action and reaction. In a game like this, it's easy for the other side to always be ahead. I told the nurses that. I said, "There's no winning when you're the underdog." They said, "You know the rules," but gave me enough toothpaste to see me through the day, to try and tempt my participation with a taste of the rewards. But I'm not that easy.

"What do you want to talk about today?"

Like he doesn't already have it planned.

"Don't you know?" I ask him.

"I only know what I want to talk about, and we'll get to that," he says.

What's going on inside my head?

"I need more than a hairbrush." Because it's really bothering me, that I don't have even the smallest requirements for living. "I need shampoo, and a razor . . ." And I don't want to use it under the supervision of one of the nurses. "And lotion. With cocoa butter, so I smell like I'm at the beach."

"The things you had on the outside?" he asks.

"No." I'm only asking for the minimum. On the outside I had a Lady Swan razor and shower gel that smelled like jasmine.

"What else?" What else does a girl in my kind of work buy for herself?

Not much. There's never enough left over for the dream things.

"I have a pair of gold hoop earrings with dolphins dangling in the center. Fourteen carat." My prize possession.

Last year a girl I knew went to jail and she gave me her leather boots. Real leather and hardly worn. "They were a half size too big, but I wore them almost every day." Made me feel like a rich girl.

"What do you have that you can't live without?" I ask him. What wouldn't he want to give up?

"We're talking things?" he says. "Not people?"

Sure. I already know what it's like living without the one person who made life worth it.

He doesn't have to think about it. He comes up with two things. He loves old bicycles and restores them. They hang in his garage, where not even the cars are allowed to park. One dates back to the 1800s.

"So your garage is a museum?"

His wife thinks so, but she puts up with him because he's the real thing.

"We make adjustments when it's worth it," he says.

We give a little when we know the payback will be big.

"So at the end of my road there's a pot of gold?"

If I make the right decisions. If I think enough of myself to make some changes.

"You think another job is the answer?"

"No," he says. It's part of the equation but, "It's not the beginning."

My beginning is here. Now.

He's looking right at me.

My savior.

But he's shaking his head. He tells me, "The only person who can save you is you."

"Then I'm in big trouble."

"It's life or death," he says. I'll always get the truth from him.

And I'm too smart to take anything he offers wrapped up like candy.

"Choose life," he says.

My life is waiting for me. What do I want to do with it?

"It's not that easy."

"It's work," he says. "Twenty-four/seven."

It's a battle I'll wage in my mind. Do I have a fighting spirit?

It could be months before I have anything to show for it.

It's not for the weak.

He can promise me food and shelter. And support from people like him.

All at a price. But I won't have to take my clothes off for it. I'll pay with my heart.

"Then we already have a problem," I say. I cashed in my heart years ago.

He wants to create a picture. He'll speak the words and I'll draw it in my mind.

"You live behind closed doors," he says. "Right now, they're locked from the inside."

What do I see?

He'll keep knocking on the door, but he's not going to break it down. I have to open it. I have to want it if it's ever going to work.

"Really," he says, "you have nothing to lose."

I see myself in my tiny apartment, with just a sink, a toilet, and a mattress thrown on the floor; with the refrigerator half the size of me and a hot plate for boiling water; I'm standing in front of the door. *Knock. Knock. Knock.* I reach for the handle. I try to, but my arm doesn't move. I tell myself, Open it. But nothing. I'm as still as a statue.

"I can't open it," I tell him. I want to. My mind is practically screaming at my body to move.

"What are you afraid of?" he asks.

I'm afraid to move and afraid not to. And I don't like that he brought me to this place. Life is a lot easier when you just let it happen.

"Put it into words." What I'm feeling. Then we'll have something we can deal with. We can face it, wrestle it to the ground, drive a dagger through its heart.

But the fear is pressing against my throat and I can't talk.

He says it has to do with trust.

"You're afraid to trust me, but more afraid to trust yourself."

"What are you going to do about that?" I ask him.

He laughs. But he's right about me. I am afraid to trust him; I'm more afraid that it's too late. That there are too many pieces of me missing.

He says I'll be doing all the work and I may as well cut myself a break.

"You'll open that door," he says. He has faith in me.

And that's the other thing he wouldn't want to live without. Faith. It makes anything possible.

pleasure seekers

They don't always screen guests. Sometimes they're desperate to entertain us, to occupy our time until lights out, that they'll let anyone come who expresses an interest. Today it's a Gautama Buddha priest. In his orange robes he looks like a toasted marshmallow. The artificial lights glare off his shaved head.

"Have no accumulation," he says. "Be tranquil . . . free from pride. You are the envy of even the gods.

"An unpolluted lake . . . the thought is calm, the speech and action are calm. You are liberated and gone to serenity.

"Banish your compulsions and attachments and you'll be hard to track, like birds in the sky."

You mean, if I give up food and sex, I can fly away? No one will find me? You mean, if I forget all I've learned, if I close my eyes and imagine an empty world, with no johns, no Manny Marquez, or someone like him, no family life that might have been unbearable, no memory, I'll be free?

Nirvana.

He says we can attain it if we strike out for a life without cumbersome baggage. We must forget that our fathers raped us, that our babies lie breathless at the bottom of trash cans. Our lives, filled with too much indulgence, must be snuffed out. Purge ourselves of permissiveness.

Who you are, is no more. This is a new beginning. Your life is a clean slate. You may begin inscribing at any moment.

"Put your hands together," he says. "Raise them to the level of your heart. Listen to the beat. You are the lungs and the air that fills them. And nothing else . . . you are nothing else . . . nothing . . ."

Which is all well and good, if we could carry our nothing- ness to better accommodations. As it is, when we open our eyes, we are still Dolores, we are still Chloe Doe, and Mary Christine. Our addresses are zip codes. We're the Mary Magdalenes of the world.

*   *   *

"Forests are pleasant where people do not frolic; those who are free of passion will enjoy them, because they are not pleasure seekers."

According to the Great Gautama, turning tricks makes us pleasure seekers. Taking a john, saying I'll do it for fifty dollars, isn't work. It isn't paying the bills, like I've been thinking. It isn't keeping a roof over my head. Instead, it's my great passion. I'm wanting each and every john I pick up. I'm wanting them in the carnal sense. I'm a nympho. And this behavior is keeping me in shackles. I'm a prisoner of the flesh, and that never leads to any good.

He's crazy, this *chungo* man with no hair and shit for brains. He passes out leaflets called "Thousands":

1. Better than a thousand sayings composed of meaning-less statements is a single meaningful statement.
2. You may perform ritual sacrifices a thousand times every month for a hundred years and it's not so good as honoring an Enlightened One for a single moment of your lifetime.
3. It is better to live one day ethically and reflectively than to live a hundred years immoral and unrestrained.

They're like something you pull out of a fortune cookie. Only there's little hope, and no promise of making it rich anytime soon. No promise that a big change in your life is right around the corner. That you'll meet someone. That you're trusted, admired, loved. That you'll be successful in business.

That someone, a relative or friend, is about to make you happy. They're not offering us a future, something to look forward to.

He doesn't touch us. He walks by and to each one of us he bows his head. He looks at us with black eyes and doesn't smile. This is a serious business. He's looking for our *arhat,* our *alma,* our soul. But we don't have it. We're not at peace.

Before he leaves, when he's standing at the door and makes a final bow meant for all of us, doctors included, he says, "It takes years of practice to make even the Lesser Journey."

Something good has come from the Buddha's visit. In group we decide to make our own fortunes. The doctors like this idea. They think it's healthy for us to look ahead, to visualize our lives as we'd like them to be, being realistic, of course, about what we can actually achieve. The nurses help us. When one of us decides she wants to marry Leonardo DiCaprio, she's told, No, that won't do. You must be realistic. Find one thing you think you'd like about being married. You can write that on your fortune.

After hours of searching and contemplation she writes, Your hard work will pay off in the bedroom.

She's told to start again.

Another chooses to be *el presidente.* They let her down easy.

What will you do as president, they ask.

She'll open all the homes of the rich to the poor. She'll make sure all the population knows a hungry day. She'll plant trees and do away with factories.

No good. You must be realistic. Pick something else.

The little *Niña* decides she wants to lead millions of people to the Holy Land. She's the only one of us who listened to our guest. Who believes that her saving, and ours, is nothing more than a decision we make. They want us to believe in something, preferably ourselves.

The staff applauds her efforts. They tell her only she can stand in her way.

At our next group we present our futures.

When it's my turn I tell them I've put a great deal of thought into my future and have come up empty-handed. I tell them, though the world is full of opportunity, I don't think there'll be a knock at my door.

The doctors say, Chloe, of course there's going to be good in your life. If you can imagine it, you can achieve it, and all that pump-up-your-life bit they're taught in school.

I know they won't let up until I satisfy them, so I pull out my fortunes. I tell them I've made the list in preparation for life on the outside. I have three expectations:

1. You are admired for your special talents.
2. You have skills others envy.
3. Great fortune awaits you.

The doctors aren't happy with our efforts. We haven't applied ourselves. We didn't take the project seriously. We didn't think about the future; we're stuck in the past.

We were supposed to expand our horizons, without going

overboard. Broaden our scope past the familiar: What would we *like* to be?

We need to have a purpose, do we see that? A goal.

Would any of us like to go to college? There's a class offered by the state that will help us get our GED. And then there's a grant that will pay for our attendance at the community college. We can all become lab technicians or typists. We can go to work in a hospital or business. We can answer phones, greet people when they come into the office. We'd be the first line of defense. Have we thought about any of this? Would we like to learn a trade that will employ us, get us a paycheck, guaranteed, and keep us off the street?

We're all thinking, How much will it pay? Is it more than I can make in a month of Saturday nights?

That, and benefits, too. And a feeling like we're doing something worthwhile. They say, You can walk among society with your head up. You can become a member.

The Gautama left behind a legacy. The fortunes are cut out in thin strips and tacked to walls and doors. Some of them are printed on pink paper, curled like authentic Chinese cookie fortunes.

We've become realistic about our efforts. We know they're unsuccessful, that they point us in no clear direction without the belief to back them, and that's the way it's supposed to be. They're nice to read, and to hold on to for a moment, but they're not to be believed.

vons grocery

Dr. Dearborn wonders if any of us have worked a real job. I tell him, I tried it your way.

"I worked at Vons, unpacking boxes in the middle of the night." I stocked toilet paper, tampons, and Colgate toothpaste. They gave me the hygiene aisle.

"The checks were enough for rent, period."

I gave up my livelihood to starve to death? No way. When it came time to feed my stomach, I stole from the shelves. I'm not ashamed of it. There's more shame in begging on the street, or in giving up.

"I was fired for it." Not the first time. The first time they caught me they were nice. They cared about me wasting away in my apartment. They asked me, "Chloe, is there no way you can pay for these things?" And I explained my life to them. How the money they paid me goes only so far. So they told me they'd feed me while I was on the job.

But what about my days off? Do I pay my electric bill or do I eat? Enough time goes by with me sitting in the dark, eating soup straight from the can, that I start feeling less than human.

So I started doing some of the guys in the back, behind the boxes, on delivery nights.

"It wasn't a bad arrangement," I say, but the memory sticks in my throat, makes my words thin, unbelievable. I try to push through it. "I didn't have to go look for it."

"But it bothered you," he says.

The truth is I hated every minute of it. Especially the way they looked at me after, sometimes like I wasn't even there, sometimes like they wanted to wipe me off their shoes. I stopped being Chloe who stocked the girlie items and was just someone they wanted to forget.

That hurt.

"Vons paid for the extras," I tell him. "You know, the *tesoros*.

The pretty things. What I have to have. Like these earrings. They cost me twelve dollars, but they're real silver."

He doesn't look at them. He's waiting, but that's all I have. Vons was it and there's no happy ending there.

"So that was my one great attempt at the good life," I say. "That's why I know it doesn't work. Not for me."

"Are you saying you'll go back to the street?"

I'll go back because it's all I know.

Because I'm good at it.

Because it pays the bills.

"It's a vicious cycle," I tell him. "I need to eat. I need to know I won't come home to an eviction notice. The only thing that gives me that is my job. You see, Doc? Like my sister always said, it's a matter of survival.

"Soon after, the *policía* will pick me up. I'm underage. They'll say, 'Why not Madeline Parker? Give this girl a chance to change.' Then I'll be back here, looking at your smiling face."

Isn't that nice?

"You want to come back?" he asks. "Once isn't enough?"

He doesn't understand King of the Mountain. He doesn't know how I can feel like I have the world in the palm of my hand when I'm selling myself at the going rate.

He says as much. My *doctor*. He wants me to make sense of it for him.

I tell him there's no way he'll ever understand.

"Guys don't get it," I say. "Especially when they had a mom baking them pies and checking their homework. Did you have a mom like that, Doc?"

He says she was something like that. He got paid for good grades.

"Then maybe you do understand, just a little."

We were both paid for a good performance.

Let's try it, he says. Give him a chance.

"It's like I'm not even there," I tell him. It's a mindless occupation. I can go over my grocery list while I'm working.

This is how I try to explain:

It's better than doing it to a husband you've come to hate. Strangers are always a better trick.

"I bet you've had women complain they can't stand their husbands. Couldn't give them love one more time if their lives depended on it.

"Maybe even your wife, huh, Doc? Does she refuse you? Is she cold, like the North Pole?"

"Let's stay focused," he says. We're talking about Chloe Doe.

Right. Right. Chloe Doe.

We come from different circumstances. I survive, and that's what it's all about.

I tell him, "There was never any multiple choice."

"So your life was already decided? So you have no control over what you do tomorrow?" he asks.

"So you made the best of your circumstances, and turned your hovel into a palace?"

A palace? No. I wouldn't go so far as to say my hole in the wall is the Beverly Wilshire. But it's my *nido,* my home. And maybe that makes it a palace. Sure, and I'm Princess Diana come back to life.

One man's trash is another man's treasure. Right?

"So, you're happy with the arrangement?"

"It has its moments," I tell him.

"I'm happy I've got something I do good. I'm happy I've got something that pays as well as it does.

"In fact, Doc," I say, "I bet I can beat your money in a day's work. What do you say? Let me out of here for a Saturday night? I'll go out and do a little doctoring of my own. We can see who makes more in an honest day's work. What do you say?"

¡viva los vivos!

Today there's a real mariachi band. They'll play their guitars and trumpets and we will dance.

Mariachi bands are all male, and Mexicans are a passionate, easy breed. They're wearing blood-red shirts and flap their arms like rabid chickens.

We like the broad, brown faces of the men, their crooked smiles, and their hot eyes on our bodies.

They like dance here. It kills two birds with one stone. We get exercise and recreational therapy at the same time. They get to watch, to sit back and enjoy the music, to instruct or reprimand from the sidelines. For them, work is an easier day.

We have special antennae, us *amantes*. A sixth sense. We know a man from his scent. Not the cologne and sweat smell that sticks to a girl's body, but the scent of man underneath.

He's vinegar, and depending on his disposition, he's sour or he's sweet.

These mariachi men, they're all right. They're what we expect on the street, and maybe better. They have what we call religion: they'll adore you, and it lasts as long as a prayer.

You don't have to worry about them hitting you. You don't have to worry about much with men like this. They'll take their pleasure and leave you. If you're lucky, they'll make you a little slice of heaven for themselves, and there's worse you can be for a man. When you're someone's angel, you're not a whore. You're their world. A person has a way of treating their world, the best part of it, like it's something they want to go on forever. They treat you real well. They treat you like you're their Madonna. And that made it easier, my life on the street.

We worked for this. Every Tuesday and Thursday in the gym for a month, with our recreational therapist, we learned the seductive moves of the dance. The mariachi will play their music and serenade us, and we will dance around them in bright skirts and white blouses the staff donated for the event from their own closets.

Our audience is the doctors who examine us, who peel back our flesh for a look at our insides; the nurses who herd us from one activity to another, confusing our names and ailments; and the social workers who can't imagine our experiences, who place us in recovery groups for problems we don't have.

They're standing and sitting in groups, backed up against the walls to give us space. They're watching, talking among themselves, waiting with their arms crossed over their stomachs, passing time until we begin.

For them we learned the hopping, laughing hyena steps of this dance. For their entertainment, we'll perform.

The mariachis begin the light strumming of their guitars and the triumphant blasts of their horns. They drift around the room, first impressing the nurses in their pant uniforms, and then the doctors who sit in folding chairs at the edge of our dance floor. They play and bow their slim bodies toward the women, smiling.

Mexicans have something we don't. I've seen it in my *chicas* on the street, in the men who buy us, in the mariachi who play. It's in their smile: life is for the living. ¡*Viva los vivos!*

For the hours of TV, for our choice of chocolate cake for dessert, for a check mark next to Cooperative on our charts, we dance. We dance because it's expected. Because the men have come for the women to dance.

95

The mariachi, their eyes speak. They tell us *unas muchachas bonitas*. Pretty girls. Pretty girls with pretty breasts and thighs like sweet cream. And there's expectation, like the shiny blade of a knife. These girls will dance, they will open themselves to our loving. Optimism is their only fault.

They watch me, flung out and arms stretched above my head, turning and turning. They watch the nurses and the doctors, sitting in their folding chairs, feet pumping to the music, their eyes watching the mariachi and watching me and watching the others. But mostly watching me. If I go on, spinning, if I lose my balance and fall, all of this will be for nothing. If I spread myself out, lay myself down, if I lose myself completely, this goes belly-up.

There's only so far you can go in America without being *gringo*. There's only so much work the mariachi will put into defeat. I would be their finest achievement, but I'm watched like a convict.

The mariachi turn their attention to the others. The girls move sluggishly to the tempo, uninvolved in the freewheeling journey I'm on. They lift their feet: sleepwalkers. Like a merry-go-round, they get nowhere. Even those who try to keep up, trip over a chord. And the rest, they wait for a loud noise. They wait for the mariachi to scatter like crows. The little Niña especially. She is jumpy around men. She won't sit behind a closed door with her therapist. She won't make eye contact with any of the male staff unless she's forced to. It's written as one of her goals: The little Niña will, when speaking to a male staff member, make eye contact on two out of three occasions. They don't expect perfection. Which is a good thing. The little Niña would never measure up. Now, she twirls in a circle by herself, at the edge of the dance floor. She stares at her feet, lifting them one beat behind the music. She refuses to look at the mariachi, or at anyone else.

The mariachi notice her and leave her to herself. They weave themselves around the rest of us, playing their instruments. They brush against us. An elbow touches a breast. A hip brushes our *nalgas*. Anything for free.

It's happening for them, inside their bodies. They watch us lift our legs and move across the floor. Bright, black eyes watching us all the way, imagining things. Their skin flushes red. The muscles under their black chinos and ruffled blouses are tight. They want us, but will settle for watching, for painting pictures. They will find satisfaction in something small. ¡*Viva los vivos!*

"Hey, mariachi!" I hold up the hem of my skirt. I dance my way across the floor, working to the music. "Mariachi!" I can dance. My body moves on the beat. I'm in tune. My mouth open, laughing. My white teeth dazzling. "Mariachi, come dance with me!"

Chloe Doe is the master of movement. In dance, I'm graceful. I move like water downstream. I'm lovely.

In invitation, I'm obvious. There's one I'm interested in. So young, his skin is smooth. No beard, not even the start of one. A pencil-thin, wannabe mustache. And skinny. *Palo*. A stick. The way I like them. I dance a circle around him. He laughs and stomps his foot, and plays his guitar faster. My heels follow his lead. They stop and watch, the other *amantes*. They clap their hands and start to chant: "Chloe! *¡OLÉ!* Chloe! *¡OLÉ!*"

The doctors and nurses are caught off guard. They stand and move closer and are frozen, trying to find a way to restore order. They all watch me, because Chloe in motion is mesmerizing.

¡Viva los vivos! I glow with it.

The mariachi men smile and nod their heads. They pick at their guitars with blunt fingers. They run a bow over a violin. They throw their heads back and laugh with delight. They are men of dance and men of music, and men of food and of women, of passions.

They're not complicated. Not difficult to understand. The mariachi men can be reduced to one thing only: *esperanza.* Hope.

We are born with it. Some with less than others. And these consume it, or they wither and die. I'm a consumer. I know it. I eat it out of their hands. I see it in their eyes and I'm snagged.

"Mariachi, I'm watching you." I dance away from the skinny guitar player. I look at him with big eyes and satisfaction. "I like what I see."

I back off before the doctors and nurses come. I drop the hem of my skirt and spin away to the corner of the dance floor. Some of the girls begin to step into the rhythm. The guitar player watches me. His eyes follow me around the floor, where I turn and laugh and hold the hem of my skirt above my knees so my legs move smoothly through each pump and twist of the dance.

*   *   *

When the mariachi leave, we are called to sit in a circle, in folding chairs. All seventeen of us. The doctors, Dr. Dear included, sit with legs crossed and with pens and clipboards ready. They want feedback, to know what we think of today's activity.

Dr. Dearborn says, "That was fun," and waits for our response.

Only the little Niña will talk. She says, "The music was nice." But she didn't like the dancing. "I have two left feet."

Chloe, they say, you had fun?

"Oh, yeah, I love dancing."

And the men. The attention, the spotlight. We like knowing they wanted us.

They doubt my word. They say, "Sometimes we hold on to the familiar because it's all we know."

hand tricks

I'm late. I sat on my bed and watched the big hand on the plastic travel-size clock tick-tick past ten. At ten-oh-eight the floor nurse comes in asking did I forget.

I didn't.

Individual therapy is not voluntary, she says.

She walks me down the hall. "What's the matter with you?"

She thought I was over this refusal. I've been in ten weeks now. One month in I played possum with the flu and skipped two sessions. I needed time to think. Time to accept my change of address. To decide I was worth the work, the sacrifice, the walking through quicksand.

"I thought you liked Dr. Dearborn," she says.

Not today.

"What's so special about today?" she wants to know. Why the sudden change of heart. "It usually takes a girl to the three-month mark before she realizes the road ahead is almost too much."

"I'm a fast learner," I say. It's true. I thought a lot about our last visit and how I was held prisoner inside my own mind, and I don't know if I can live up to expectations. I don't know if I want to try. I've lived scared so long, I'm a natural. Rule number one: don't let the fear catch you, and now he wants me to turn around and stare it in the face. That may be more than I can do.

We stop in front of the library and she knocks, all the gold bracelets on her arms sounding like wind chimes.

"There you go, now," she says. She pushes the door open and nudges me through it.

"Chloe." Dr. Dear is smiling like I'm a long-lost friend. "It's good to see you."

I sit down in my chair. Let my lip curl at the stink of his words.

"You want to talk about it?" he asks.

"It's like you said," I tell him. "Two steps forward, one back."

"You're slipping?" he guesses. "How?"

"Not slipping," I say. "It feels more like being stuck in one place and not liking the scenery."

"You want out?"

In a way. I want that place where time stops, where there's zero gravity and I'm a floater. Except for bumping into a few things, no one's there to bother me.

"It's getting harder," he says. His face is all soft with understanding, but this just makes me want to sharpen my nails on his pink-white skin, leave a mark of my own. "You're thinking you can't do it."

"Something like that."

"What does your gut tell you?"

"I haven't been able to eat for days," I tell him. Nothing goes down and stays. I'm a case of nerves, damned if I do and if I don't.

"So let's take it easy today," he says. He won't poke at anything real personal. We'll leave family alone, and even the here and now, and work on the future. What do I see for myself?

Where am I going? And, please, be *realistic*.

But that's the one thing I can't be. Reality hurts worse than possibility.

"You want me to say I'm headed nowhere." I'm traveling a dead-end street. "Chances are, going the way I am, I'll end up in jail." Or dead.

He wants me to say it. He wants it bad enough he's willing to steer me in the direction of the morgue.

"Chloe, most girls don't last long on the street." They don't last.

He watches how I'm taking it. Pushes his glasses up his nose to make sure he doesn't miss a thing.

Am I going to crack? Am I going to give him what he wants? A few tears.

None of this is new to me. He forgets I was the one out there. I saw the girls disappear like a magician's hand trick. Only they didn't come back. Girls like me are not pulled out of a hat or a sleeve. When we disappear we're gone for good.

The doctor asks, "So what happens to them?"

He wants me to say they're dead. But I won't. He wants me to say, I know where they are. All those unmarked graves, they're girls like me. But I can't.

"They come here. The Hospitality Inn."

Here is only a resting place. Here is where you collect yourself. You were one small step from falling over the edge, and then you came here. When you leave you're ready for just about anything. Maybe you're ready to believe.

"Where are you going, Chloe?"

"I have plans," I tell him. "I have friends. My *cuates* are waiting for me."

"Share your plans with me," he says. "Where will you be a month after you're out? Six months? A year from the day you leave Madeline Parker, where will you be?"

Have you thought about it? Have you planned ahead?

But I haven't. Really, there's no one waiting for me. On the street everything is temporary, even life.

I feel like I'm six feet under, that all the air has been squeezed from my lungs. My fingers curl into my palms until I feel the sting of my nails digging into my skin and I know I am alive. But that's not what he wants. He led me here, hoping for a change in attitude. Hoping an up-close at my name on the list of the dead would bring a willingness to start new.

I don't want to play his game today.

"I think I'll get an apartment on the beach. Live like the rich and famous."

"That's expensive real estate," he says.

He's disappointed. Today I'm being irreverent. He uses the big word on me, thinking I don't understand it. He skipped over the part in my file that says I'm a born genius. That in grades three through six I attended special classes. And when the state had ahold of me, I was on the honor roll.

"And flippant, too," I agree.

Something snaps in his eyes and I see I've been caught. He knew all along, but he turns it into a game.

"Insolent."

"Supercilious," I say.

"Impudent."

"You got a thing for I's?"

"Exasperating." And his eyes bug behind his glasses.

I like seeing him like this. Sometimes I get on my own nerves; I've never had a shrink tell me I was pressing on his.

"So, you think I'll be dead?" I say, and I really consider this. If I haven't thought about it, if I can't do it myself, then someone else will.

"If you don't start taking yourself seriously," he says.

"And you, too, huh?"

"You take me seriously. And it scares you."

I feel my eyes dry up with the pressure of looking at him. My hands twitch from wanting so much to move them.

"What do you have that can scare me?"

He holds out his hand, palm up, and taps it with a finger. "Your life. Do you want it?"

heat wave

Before the sun is completely gone, the moths come out. Swarms of them. They settle on the porch lights and if they stay too long, we hear the snap-burn of their bodies. In the morning we scrape them off the glass. Last year Camille and I made a house for them out of a plastic jug and cut grass, then caught them. If you don't let them go by morning, they die.

This year we forget about their reaction to captivity and do it all over again.

"Mr. Portsmith's mowed his lawn," Camille says. Mr. Portsmith's mower doesn't have a grass catcher. "We can go over now. He's inside having iced tea."

We walk over to where our yards border and scoop up handfuls of cut, brown grass. It's been a dry year and June has hit us hard, with record temperatures and the air so sharp it chokes us going down. There's been so little rain, the news warns us we may have to give up drinking water from our faucets. The government asks us to bathe in three inches of water and not to take showers. Our mother tells us to flush the toilet only when there's something in there no one else would want to look at. I take that to mean every time I go. Camille says it's only when we do number two, but she flushes every time. I hear her.

This year we take an old shoe box: Converse, black high-tops, size eleven. They belonged to one of our mother's boyfriends. We don't remember who. We make a bed of grass and Camille puts in red rose petals from our bushes. We use a piece of clear wrap for the lid, cut small slits in the plastic so the moths can breathe, then wander around under the streetlights.

Camille looks like a drunk, swaying and grabbing at the air.

Last year we filled the jug. We had thirty of them. They don't light up like fireflies, or rub their legs together, singing, like grasshoppers do. They don't beat their wings, frantic for escape. They lay quietly, one on top of another, and fall into a deep sleep.

Camille says they smothered each other. There were too many of them. Or they died from the heat of too many bodies. We went to sleep with the jug on the nightstand between our beds and the light on, and when we woke up in the morning, they were shriveled up on the bottom.

Today they're killing the man who hurt little boys. Who dragged them off to empty fields and touched their private parts. Then he killed them.

"How?"

"He smashed their heads," Camille says. "He strangled them with a leather belt." Probably the one he was wearing.

"He wrapped their heads in plastic so they couldn't breathe. He's a real sick bastard."

On the evening news they show groups of people holding candles in the dark. They sing hymns and stand outside the prison gates with signs that quote the Bible: *Thou Shalt Not Kill*. And signs that say *Two Wrongs Don't Make a Right*.

Camille says they're morons. "They don't have children. Or don't like them."

They'll kill him tonight at one minute after twelve. His mother will watch from behind a glass wall.

Camille has nine moths in her box. There are less of them this year because of the heat. Nothing is surviving.

Yesterday Camille and I walked to 7-Eleven for Cokes and counted thirteen dead birds along the way. The news says to watch cats and small dogs, especially. Small animals are victims of the weather. We wore socks with our tennis shoes but still felt the heat through the rubber soles.

It's only the second week of June. School let out two days early because there were no air conditioners and the old fans just pushed hot air.

Camille says it's so hot because hell is opening up to snatch the child-killer.

In the afternoons we lay on the floor in the living room, in front of the fan, and sing our names into the whirling blades:

C-h-l-l-o-o-e-e-e

C-a-a-m-i-l-l-l-e

The curtains are drawn and the room is shadowy. We don't turn on the light. We're not allowed to open the refrigerator; our mother will get us what we need, if she thinks we really need it. We have an old blue Westinghouse refrigerator and the ice cubes are melting in the tray, even with the temperature on COOLEST and us opening it only three or four times a day.

"They're not going to make it." Camille shakes her box and the moths open their wings. They're slow and maybe ready to die.

Once, I killed one between my fingers; its body crumbled like ash and blew away. It was an accident.

"Let them go," I tell her. "They're no use to you dead."

She puts the box on the street, between her feet, and hangs her head over them, watching their lives fade.

We're sitting on the sidewalk, catching what little wind comes. Neighbors drive by and honk. Across the street, Mr. Shearer prunes his roses while Mrs. Shearer holds up a flashlight. Stars come out in the still-blue sky.

"Why don't you let them go?"

"It's natural selection," Camille explains. "Only the strong survive."

She wants to be a scientist.

The parents of the boys will watch, too. People from the news will record his last words, how he looks when the poison hits him, if he says he's sorry.

Camille says her last words would be the name of the man she loves, and she'll only kill if she has to. She'll kill if her life is in danger, or if the man she loves is about to be murdered. But she'll never kill someone's baby.

He'll struggle, Camille says. They'll tie him down, but his body will have a mind of its own.

That's why the parents come. Ten seconds of screaming pain will heal their broken hearts.

In the morning the moths are curled up on the bottom of the box, and Camille flushes them down the toilet. She says, "Thank you for the brief shining moments of your lives that touched mine," as the water swirls and is swallowed up.

The night before, Camille and I stayed up past midnight. We watched the clock from our beds, where we were supposed to be sleeping. When it was twelve-oh-one Camille said, "One less devil to worry about." But I thought the words in my mind, *Two wrongs don't make a right.*

match game

I'm here three months when he pulls out the big artillery.

"Do you want your mother to come for a visit?"

Like he knows who she is and exactly where to find her.

"Is the old address still good?"

Sure. I've been writing her letters. One every week I've been gone.

"Have you ever written her?"

He looks harmless today, in shoes that are almost worn-through in the soles. I tell him I have better walks than that, me, a guest of the state.

"You want to borrow a few dollars?" I ask him. Get yourself some shoes that won't let in the rain.

He's planning on shopping over the weekend. And thanks, but he can manage on his small county paycheck. "What was your address?" he asks again.

"I don't remember it," I tell him, even though I know the street name and number better than I do my birthday.

Sometimes I think about Gordo, the only man who was nice to us, who lived two doors down and painted his house the color of avocados when they're peeled open; that next-to-the-pit color of yellow-green, because it reminded him of a small town in Mexico where his brothers still lived.

I tell him about Gordo, because he's the only memory from that place that doesn't draw blood.

He says I remember Gordo so well because he's the only healthy male influence of my young life. And he wore his heart on his sleeve: people appreciate someone willing to feel his own loneliness.

Really? Every day without Camille is like walking without my shadow. I turn, thinking she'll be right there. Wanting it so bad a couple of times I was sure I caught a glimpse of her red hair, her white, white skin, before she faded back to memory. How do I wear that?

But I don't tell him this. Instead, I say, "Gordo and my mother were together. I saw him naked."

He looks at me through his glasses and I stare right back at him, giving nothing away.

"Sometimes that happens," he says. "Even in the best families." For example, "We walk into a bathroom without knocking." He lets that hang between us, almost like a question: Was there something more sinister going on?

I give it up. Gordo never tried to hurt me.

"You're right," I tell him. "It was an accident."

"Chloe, do you want to see your mother?"

"You think I should." But I don't see how it's going to help me. "It wouldn't be a happy reunion."

"It's an opportunity," he says. Some girls need to face their mothers, to look them in the eye and tell them what a bad job they did. He says once I let go of those feelings, once they're with their rightful owner, my wounds will close, my scars will fade. Like I have an infection in my blood and the only way I'll heal is to let the poison ooze out of me.

What he doesn't get, is that even if he finds her, even if she comes, it won't be to hold my hand and tell me how sorry she is. And, anyway, it's too late for that.

"I never wrote her," I admit, "but I called her once. I had to tell her who I was."

"She didn't forget you."

"She didn't recognize my voice." I'd only been gone a year. "And then there was silence." So much of it, I thought she had dropped the phone, or maybe I had given her a heart attack and she was on the floor gasping for breath. Later, I hoped that it was true. That she was so sorry she missed her chance to tell me the things I needed to hear, that she died. I believe that regret and sorrow can do that to a person.

"What did you need to hear?"

He knows this answer. He has kids of his own.

"That she was sorry?"

"That too."

I really wanted to know that she loved me, missed me, wanted me back.

"I did all the talking. 'Hi, Mom.' SILENCE. 'It's me, Chloe.' SILENCE. SILENCE. SILENCE. 'Chloe.' I hoped, with Walt gone, she was thinking clearer. I told her, 'I want to come home.'"

"She never spoke." I cried, I asked her to say something. Say my name. What's my name, Mom? "She hung up."

"And that was the end of it?"

"You know I feel like a bug with a pin through my heart?" The way he looks at me nonstop.

"Too intense?"

"I feel like I can't move."

He tells me I can get up, walk around.

Like a fly buzzing around inside a bottle. I can't leave. The only out comes when he twists off the cap and turns me upside down. Until then I'll feel the air grow thinner, become weightless in my lungs. Sometimes he keeps me until I almost pass out and the world is white.

"So?" he says. "You never talked to her again?"

"Yeah, sure I did. I called back a few weeks later and told her all the things you think I need to tell her. So, you see, it's been done. I guess I know a little about doctoring.

"I have nothing to say to her."

I shift. The chair is tight. Feels tighter. I pull at my hospital-issued V-neck cotton shirt. Three meals and snacks, too. I never ate this good.

"You can come up with a few words."

When I think of my mother, my heart's a flat line.

"You feel something," he insists. "Don't you ever just want to scream?"

I feel like my body's been raging for years.

He likes my analogy, that prostituting my body has really been my way of exorcising my anger. It's self-destructive but the only way I know to keep my engine running. And my mother had self-destructive behaviors, too.

Yeah? "Like what?"

He watches me a moment, taking off his glasses and folding them into the palm of his hand.

"She had a lot of men in her life," he points out. "Like you."

"Not really." The men in my life are just passing through. None stay long enough it hurts.

I am not my mother. I'm not anything like her.

I look around the room. Chairs, a bookshelf, a table with

names and body parts carved into the wood. Not even a window. There'll be no escaping today. No leaping from the flames and sprinting into the crowd.

I wait him out. I won't look at him, won't break the silence. I hear him move; his crossed leg comes undone and his foot hits the floor. He inches forward in his chair.

"That bothers you. A lot."

Good work, Sherlock.

"You're a smart girl, Chloe," he says. "You thought about this before."

"I'm not like my mother." I have thought about this, and there are some important differences. For starters, the only damage I do is to myself.

"There are some differences," he agrees.

But not many. He won't say it because he won't argue. Some truths, he told me, need to be realized if they're going to be worth anything.

"So you think we're a pair." I have to clear my throat and his eyes go soft. I don't want him feeling sorry for me. I put the anger I'm feeling in my eyes and lay them on him. "Like mother, like daughter."

"I think she made it too easy for you to take to the streets. To think of it as your only choice."

Promiscuity starts at home.

He sees a pattern. My mother's willingness to share her body with a number of men in return for what she thought was love is similar to me paying my bills and putting food in my stomach. I can see that. There was more money when my mother had a man around, more food in the cupboards.

And I thought she didn't teach me a thing.

"What else?" I want to know the other ways he compared us and found a match.

"She put up a good fight," he says, "trying to ignore that what she was doing to herself, to her girls, was fatal."

I never held another person's life in my hands and then shook them loose.

"What did it feel like," he wants to know, "going to your mother, asking her for help, and she turned you away?"

She needed Walt more than she needed us. "The only thing I need from the *cachas* is money. My mother couldn't live without love."

"Is that what she had with your stepfather?"

"She thought so." And she believed she'd never find it again.

"Your mother loved her husband more than she did you," he spells it out.

"Even though he was a dirtbag," I agree.

"Even though he hurt you," he adds. "She loved him."

That's right. She didn't want to believe he hurt us, even when the truth was the only thing left in the room.

"And you felt . . ."

I wait a beat and lift my shoulders.

"You going to make this multiple choice?"

He says they have to be my words. I have to take ownership of my feelings.

"You realized your mother wasn't going to come through. You were on your own."

How did I feel then?

I try not to think of that moment. Every time I do it wraps around my throat, takes a bite out of me. But he's waiting, his eyebrows perched above the silver rims of his glasses and looking like he could stay exactly where he is another day or two.

The look on her face was like being pushed off a cliff. "It was a long fall and knowing the whole way I was dying."

He smiles real big and toothy, like a pumpkin.

"That's good," he says. We made progress today.

"She should have loved you better." Just in case I didn't know it. If no one ever said it to me before.

She should have saved me. And Camille. Think about how different my life would be then.

"And Hitler never should have happened." So long as we're dreaming.

"She's the reason you're here," he says. "Do you see that?"

I do, but I gave him enough. He's happy and too old to be doing cartwheels. Besides, I need to keep a little something for myself.

high dive

This summer our mother is working at the city pool for extra money. Camille and I get in for free. And we get free licorice whips, we both like black, and Coke, but only one cup each. We have to wait until we're really thirsty. Sometimes we wait until our mouths are so dry it's hard to talk. The water in the fountain tastes like rust, like it's been sitting there all winter, and Camille says it can probably kill you if you already have a cold or stomach flu. She learned in school that stagnant water breeds disease.

I'm eleven years old and tall enough that I can use the high dive. You have to be twelve. Camille says she'll tell on me, but she never does. Even at thirteen she doesn't use the high dive, because she gets dizzy on the tenth step and has to push her way back down, through the bigger kids who call her chicken and peck at her, flapping their arms.

She says I'm fearless because I'm young. But in a few years I won't like heights or small places; I'll be like her friend, Mary Witcher, who's afraid of dogs and thunder and of dying in a car crash.

I know I'll always love to dive; it's like flying. It's where no one can touch me.

Sometimes I think I'm a bluebird, hanging in the air, putting off for as long as I can the time when I have to return.

Even birds can't fly forever.

I have big dreams. I'll be a world-class diver. I'll go to the Olympics. I can do a swan with a half twist; the lifeguard says that's a good start.

Our father was a swimmer. Camille says he taught both of us to swim when I was three years old, which is why I don't really remember. I only know I've been able to swim forever. Now I know my father's hands were under my stomach when I kicked to get to the side and hold the blue rail, thinking my life depended on getting there as fast as I could. I have fragments of memory: pieces of our father, but it could have been someone else. I have only Camille to tell me if I'm wrong. Most times she's pretty good at it.

I don't remember his face. Or his voice. I don't know if he cheered us on, but I think he must have, or I wouldn't love it like I do. I wouldn't be a natural.

He's what I think about when I'm up here, when I'm tumbling through the air, when everything's perfect. And I still ask Camille about him.

"What did he look like?"

"He wore blue trunks," Camille says. "And a white cap."

I've never seen a man wear a cap, but Camille says he did it for his ears. "He got a lot of ear infections."

"Did he like to dive, too?

Camille thinks there was only a small board then. She remembers he walked slowly to the very end of it, balanced on his toes, and closed his eyes like he was praying. When he did dive, there was nothing spectactular about it. Nothing like we see on the TV. Our father, Camille says, didn't have a lot of flair. We think this is one of the things that bothered our mother.

Camille was five when he left us. She knows our mother was not easy to live with.

"She yelled every time he came home, sometimes late and the dinner was ruined, sometimes early and it wasn't ready yet, and what does he expect of her if he can't give her a schedule to work on?"

Camille is good at being our mother and reliving those last days. Otherwise, I wouldn't know what was what.

"He just couldn't get it right," Camille says. "And that was it.

He stopped trying. You can't expect a man to stay around if there's no winning."

Sometimes I look at our father's picture and try to remember him. In the picture he's standing in front of our house on India Street, and the lawn is spread out in front of him. He's holding a silver thermos under his arm and wearing work clothes with splotches of paint and a tear at the elbow. It's a green shirt, and underneath, where his bony elbow sticks out, he's wearing a white thermal. He has skinny legs. The belt at his waist makes his pants bunch. The soles of his boots are worn to almost nothing. He's looking into the camera and I know his eyes are brown, because Camille told me.

Camille says I look more like him than she does. I have my father's brown eyes. Camille says he always looked hungry, and I have the same kind of thinness; a down-to-bone look that people find alarming.

Camille resembles our father in temperament. Our mother says Camille could challenge a mule in stubbornness and win nine times out of ten, "just like your father." Our mother says she knows only one other person than Camille to make up their mind so quick and permanent, our father.

I think I remember hearing him call us into dinner. I think he may be the shadow setting the table, drinking coffee, reading the newspaper to us, singing along to a Johnny Mathis Christmas album. But Camille says I want it so bad, I'm dreaming it, and this could be equally true.

On the back of his picture our father wrote:

Dad
India St.
1991

I move like I'm gravity, like it's not a decision.

Standing on my toes, on the edge of the high dive, the water looks as clear and blue as the sky.

In my head there's the possibility that this moment isn't here yet, that maybe I'm not born. I could be an idea. Or I could be realized, and life is standing still. For this moment, the world has stopped.

I have perfect balance. The wind moves around me. My heart is as light and bright as the sun. I am as light as a sparrow bone, and for one moment I am everything that can't be caught and held.

Then I'm passing through the air, turning, arms drawn in, toes pointed. My chin rests on my chest. I believe I have a chance at anything: one full revolution.

I spread my wings. I arch my back. I remember why swans are graceful, why someone would name this for something beautiful.

I think I'm touching the clouds. For a long time they keep me from breaking the blue. I don't hear the shattering surface. I belong behind this sky, all-silent and calm, and part of the world where butterflies live after they give up their feet and dream of flight. I can stay, if I pretend the fire in my chest doesn't burn, if I pretend the world is upside down, if I pretend water is the air I breathe.

supergirl

I knock once and push the door open. He's on the phone, his cell, and looks at his watch. I'm two minutes early. I didn't wait to be called today and then eat up precious minutes as I used the bathroom and then shuffled down the hall. I've been waiting all week for this session. He waves me in and then pats the back of a chair as if to say, Go 'head, sit here.

I do.

He stands with one hand in the pocket of his Dockers. He says yes into the phone several times. He calls his wife honey.

"Sorry about that," he says, and drops his cell into his coat pocket.

"Your girlfriend?"

She used to be. He married her fourteen years ago.

"Your social life is cutting into my time," I tell him.

"You're early."

"Does that get me any points?"

It does with him. "What do you want to talk about today?" He sits down, shifts his long legs so he can use one as a table, and picks up my file.

"I did a lot of thinking," I tell him. After the last time, when he told me I was a lot like my mother. I made a list of the ways we're different: I don't like makeup; I don't read love stories and think it'll happen to me; I'm not waiting for good things to come my way.

"I'm more realistic than that."

"So long as you believe you can be happy," he says.

We can all be happy. It's just a matter of taking charge of our lives.

"So, you see," I point out, "you weren't right. Not a hundred percent."

"No one ever is," he agrees.

"And there's something else. It's big."

I'm proud of myself, and happy that the things I do have in common with my mother only look that way on the outside. Dig a little deeper and I'm one of a kind.

He wants me to explain this.

"Our motivations." I use the word he's been preaching about from the beginning. I'm starting to believe that our lives are a series of decisions. "I know I got to where I am today because I decided to leave my mother's house. I know I left my mother's house because I couldn't live with the decisions others made."

It's so easy and I knew it all along, I just never thought about it.

"And this," he says, "leads us to the very real difference between you and your mother."

I wait for him to fill me in, but he says, "Why don't you tell me what it is."

I can't find the word he already knows.

It's a feeling inside me, what gets me up in the morning, what pushes me through the day.

"And what is that? What makes you able to deal with your life?"

I live off the knowledge that what happened to us, to me and Camille, was a crime. I feel closer to her on days that are really bad.

"Courage," he says.

I know the difference between right and wrong. What happened in that house was wrong, so I left.

For some people it's not that easy. Some people can't live what they believe in.

He says I'm one of a kind. I'm brave. Until now I was just doing what had to be done, but all along I've really been a hero. The way he said it, makes me feel above all the stuff that's happened, like it can't touch me. I'm caped and repel bullets. I'm Supergirl.

"And since we're already on the subject, let's dig a little deeper," he adds.

He wants to know about my first time. The first time I took a john. What moved me to do it? What shifted inside me that made the decision one I could live with?

"You ruined a beautiful moment," I tell him.

He says, "We can create another." In fact, he's looking forward to a lot of triumphs where I'm concerned.

"Small victories," I say. He really likes his idea of life being either a win or a loss.

"That's right." He smiles. "So, your first time."

"I don't kiss and tell," I say. I have more class than that.

He says I went into hiding, that first time, and never came out. He wants to meet the real Chloe. He thinks she's worth our time and that I might even like her so much I'll want her to stick around.

"What's there to like about her?"

"She's strong, and honest, and wasn't afraid to love her sister or herself." After all, she's the one who decided to leave in the first place.

"You can't love yourself if you're selling to the highest bidder,"

I remind him. The first time he said this to me I didn't believe it. Now I know it's true. I hated every time, every john, and got through it knowing I'd eat one more day, that I wouldn't sleep outside that night. After a while, I started hating that it meant so much to me, living. I suppose that is hating yourself.

He says I'm still two girls living inside one skin. And that's good for me. Once I give it up, once I let her go, I can't be saved. My soft center is the Chloe I was born to be; the outer shell, as thick as armor, is the girl I was forced to become.

I tell him he should be a poet. But I like the picture he gave me. It feels right.

"The first night I left, I didn't sleep," I tell him. "The only thing I remember about it is walking." I kept moving. I knew enough not to take the freeway; the cops would pick me up and dump me back on my mother's doorstep. So I took back roads, until I heard the ocean. "Then I walked on the sand. Miles. The sun came up and I read a sign that said SOLANA STATE BEACH." I didn't get very far.

"I didn't sleep the second night, or the third. It was pure daylight when my body broke down. I think I fell asleep walking."

I woke up because water was dripping on my face. I thought it was blood. That Walt found me and carved me up with the knife that hung from the chain on his belt. But it was a guy in a wet suit and he kept asking me, "Are you OK?"

I grabbed my backpack and took off.

"It got easier after that," I say. "After that, I started looking for a place to sleep. Usually the beach during the day. I blended in better." But the cops showed up there, too. Wanted to know why I wasn't in school. Skipping class to soak up some rays was a bad idea. They let me go, telling me if I kept it up the only job I'd get would be at McDonald's."

Turns out I couldn't even get a job there. Not that I asked for one. You need a phone for that kind of job. Even I knew that. You need a place to take a shower. To do your hair. You have to be presentable.

"You were right about my mother making it easier for me," I say. "I thought about all the times we were close to hunger, and then my mother came home with some *hombre* with a thick wallet and it was cheeseburgers for dinner."

It was always cheeseburgers the first night. And she put something green on our plates, too. Peas or green beans. Like she did a good job making sure we had vegetables. After a while that stopped, but the burgers always showed up. I couldn't get them out of my mind. I hung out in front of McDonald's, Carl's Jr., Jack in the Box the first weeks I was on my own.

"I wasn't a trash-picker. Not right away."

The first time I asked, they gave me a burger free. After that it was, NO VAGRANTS. They called the police. A girl my age, one guy said, shouldn't be on her own.

"You eat fast food, Doc? You ever eat everything that comes in your bag?"

He says he doesn't. He orders at the Drive-Thru and then parks and munches on his lunch. When he tosses his scraps into the trash, there are french fries at the bottom of his bag that he never touched. Usually some burger left, too.

I tell him, Thank you. There's someone out there who appreciates that.

"So, you were on the street how long before you sold yourself?"

I didn't at first. "I held out as long as I could."

"How long was that?"

"Longer than you think." The city got in the way. "I was on the street two months when the cops picked me up. They put me in a foster home with a mom and a dad and seven other kids like me. I didn't fit in."

"Why?"

I shrug. "The whole thing was wrong. I wanted it to be me and Camille and it was never going to be that again. I wasn't ready to let her go. I saw a guy like you, and he kept telling me not to ruin this good thing I've got going. But a home without Camille isn't a home for me. And that's why none of them worked out. Why they kept trying me out in new places. A year and a half of that and I was done."

My second time out on the street I was thirteen; I'd been there before. I knew what to expect. I slept in doorways or behind trash bags. There are rats in the city. Real ones. They crawled across my feet. Even had one sniffing my hair.

"I couldn't do it anymore," I tell him. "It's not how humans are supposed to live." I mean, no one would choose it.

"My first john was so old his hands shook. I had to help him unzip his pants."

He was parked in his car, a white Caddie, with the window rolled down. Waiting. I was on the street long enough then; I knew how it worked. I watched and listened and used the words I heard other *chicas* like me use. Hey, mister, *abuelo,* you want some of this? He looked at me a long time. He said I was sweet, so sweet, but he took me anyway.

We drove in his car until he found a street with houses and parked away from the lights.

I cried. Not because I didn't want to give him head, which is what he asked for, but because I knew the minute I left him I'd eat a real meal. The number two at Mickey D's. Quarter Pounder, fries, and a soda."

That's what it came down to for me. I wanted a meal. A hot meal that was mine, from start to finish. I wanted that more than I wanted to wake up the next morning.

So that was it, my first time.

I can see my sad story got to him. Maybe he's thinking about his wife, or his own girl. But no, he's thinking of me. No one should have to choose between that kind of life and death.

He wonders if it was easier, because Walt already took what I wanted to keep for myself. What I thought I would hold on to until I met the man of my dreams. Something secret, wrapped in white satin, like a wedding dress.

"I gave it up," I said. "And that's always better than having it stolen."

He understands this. "The power of choice, even when it's the lesser of two evils."

That's right.

graceland

Our mother met Walt Atwater when she took a package trip to Las Vegas. They sat next to each other at the slot machines. Neither of them won any money, but they had a lot of fun trying. Our mother brought thirty dollars in rolled quarters. Walt had his payroll check: "They cash it for you right there. Hand you over a roll of bills or casino chips. Any way you like it."

It took them three hours to run out of money. After that, they sat talking and drinking coffee until our mother's bus was ready to leave. Walt followed her all the way home from Las Vegas because he fell in love with her over the cherry-cheese danish and her stories of heartbreak.

Our mother says she told him so much about herself because she thought she'd never see him again.

He already knows our names and exactly what we look like. He guesses who we are, even though I'm as tall as Camille. He comes right up to us and says, "You're Camille. Yep. The red hair. So you must be Chloe. Your name means flower-in-bloom in Greek."

"What does my name mean?"

"Camille . . . Camille . . . ," he says, but the best he can come up with is, "It's a flower, of course." And we already knew that.

"Do you girls like flowers?"

Camille tells him about the rosebushes in the backyard. They were already here when we rented the place, and we water them when we remember. There's also an azalea bush that isn't doing too well.

"I have a green thumb," he says. "We'll see what's ailing it. See if we can't make it happy."

Our mother knows Walt two weeks when they go back to Las Vegas and get married in the Graceland Chapel. On the marriage certificate there's a picture of Elvis, the date — July 1st — and the names of two witnesses my mother met two minutes before the ceremony.

"He's a good man," our mother says. "He came looking for me. That's a six-hour drive." She tells us Walt had to go out of his way to get her. "It wasn't a trip to the corner market.

"A man doesn't go to that much trouble on a whim." He's serious about us. And, she wants us to know, he came for her and her girls. He knew about us from the start.

"I told him first thing, 'I have two daughters. They're as different as night and day. Chloe, she's my conscience. My oldest, well, she reminds me of me.'

"You know what Walt said? He said, 'If they're as pretty as you, you have yourself a dream come true.'"

She holds out her hand and shows us the ring he gave her. It's silver with an amethyst stone. "You see that? Walt gave that to me. It's not dime-store quality, either. That stone's semiprecious." It's her birthstone.

When they get back from Las Vegas, we ask our mother what it was like, getting married in the Graceland Chapel.

"It's small," our mother says. "There are pictures of Elvis, of course. The whole ceremony took five minutes." She waves us away with her hand. "There's not much to tell."

Walt doesn't have a job because he gave up everything when he followed his heart. Our mother says he can get back to doing what he was doing in Nevada, and she helps him look through the newspaper.

"What does Walt do?" I ask.

"He drove a truck for the Miller Brewing Company," our mother says. "We'll see if they'll hire him back. Give him a route here."

Camille tells me Walt is on her bad side. He's her enemy. Her *muñón*. Which means, he's what's left after an arm or a leg's been torn off in a terrible accident. We learned the word from our mother's friends. Camille says Walt is like Manolo, who was killed walking the tracks up from Mexico. His ghost with no arms haunts all his friends, hanging on for a taste of life.

"Why don't you like Walt?"

He touched her, pulled her against him and pushed his hand down her shorts when she was outside watering the azalea.

Camille said he was like a rabid dog, breathing down her neck.

"What did you do?"

"I bit him. I'd have bit his ear off, except I wanted to get away from him."

He left a hand mark on her skin. You can see where his fingers pressed into her, under her underwear.

We find our mother in the kitchen, emptying a box of dried potatoes into a pot on the stove. She's still wearing the blue corduroy skirt and white blouse she wore to work this morning. She looks over at us when we come in.

"What do you girls want? You come in here to help me?" She keeps her concentration on stirring the potatoes and milk.

"We came to show you something," I say.

"Oh, yeah. And what's that? You find something out in that yard? Some buried treasure maybe? That's what I'd like to see."

"No," I say. Our mother is always looking for a windfall. She says, every time she buys a lottery ticket, "Lord, let this be my windfall." Or, "Pick a number girls. Bring me luck. Bring me my pot of gold."

"Well, what do you have?" she says. She turns her eyes on us. Our mother's eyes are the prettiest we've ever seen, women in magazines included.

Camille moves closer to her and pulls down the waistband of her shorts. She shows our mother the bruise shaped like a hand that Walt left on her.

"Who the hell did that?" our mother asks. She puts the spoon down and takes hold of Camille's shorts, bending for a closer look. "Have you been roughhousing with those boys down the street? I told you to stop playing with them."

"It wasn't the boys," I say. We don't play with them.

"Well, then?" our mother asks. I look at Camille and see her eyes are beginning to tear. "Who did it?" It seems suddenly Camille can't say a word. "Damnit, girl, who left that mark on you?"

"Walt," Camille says, pulling in air like she's been running. "He came after me out by the azalea."

"What do you mean? He came after you like how?"

"Like he was a wild dog," I say, and our mother looks at me with a sharpness in her eyes and tells me to "keep quiet this minute."

136

"What'd you do?" she asks Camille. "Did you say something to him?"

"No." Camille's back straightens, like it does when she's had enough. "I was picking off those dead leaves and he came up behind me. He held me close." Like a lover, Camille said. And he wouldn't let her go.

Our mother's hand on the shorts loosens and the elastic snaps against Camille's skin. She crosses her arms over her stomach and looks down at us for a moment in silence. Her eyes look like drops of paint in her small face.

"Men don't know their strength," our mother says softly. "It was an accident." She runs her hands down the front of her skirt. "They're really just sweethearts, you know?"

But Camille isn't done. She looks our mother straight in the face and says, "He put his hand in there."

"In where? Jesus, Camille, in where?"

"In my underpants. He put his hand in my *underpants.*" And then he said to her, Jesus Christ, Camille, you have something growing there. And laughed.

Our mother takes hold of Camille's bunched fists and squeezes them gently. There's a softness about our mother's face that smoothes out the lines around her mouth. That makes her pretty. Camille says this is her payday look. When she's able to make the rent and the electric bill. But it's also how she looks when she's in love.

"Come on, now, Camille. It was an accident. We know it was an accident." She drops Camille's hands and goes back to the stove. "Well, these are burnt." She grabs the pot and carries it to the sink. "Go back outside now," she tells us.

We decide we should run away. We pack our clothes, Camille's box of lipsticks, and my book on wild horses into plastic bags we got from the grocery store. We get as far as the corner when Camille has to go back for her radio, which can run on batteries. She sits on the edge of her bed, trying to find a station. She lets her bag slip to the floor. She looks like she might stay awhile, so I remind her of what we were doing.

"We have nowhere to go," she says. And no money. We couldn't even get on the train.

evening rose

Walt takes us to Denny's for ice cream. He smells like Fritos and wears a blue shirt with his name on the pocket. He has a key ring on his belt loop and a tattoo of a woman in a red dress on his arm. When he flexes his muscles the woman dances. He got it in Mexico.

At Denny's we're allowed to order whatever we want, so long as we can finish it. Camille orders a banana split with extra strawberries. I order a mint chocolate sundae. Walt drinks coffee with two sugars and watches us eat.

Outside, the heat ripples off the pavement. It's August and Camille and I go to the Y while our mother works during the day. Sometimes Walt comes for us and takes us away from there, where we really don't want to be, where there are only little kids and poor kids whose parents can't pay for a real vacation or a babysitter. We go to the beach and sometimes ride the roller coaster. Other times, we go to Denny's.

"You have a chocolate syrup mustache," Walt tells Camille.

He asks the waitress for more napkins and puts them down in front of us.

Camille wipes her lip with her spoon and ignores him.

Camille is good at pretending not to notice people. She doesn't say hello to Walt when he comes in from work.

In the evening he and our mother sit in front of the TV and laugh. Walt does the commercials, "Pine-fresh scent with Lysol," in a woman's high-pitched voice.

"How do you like that, Camille?" he'll say, and Camille will carry on like she didn't hear anything.

I get up and leave the room, go outside with a book and let our cat, Simon, curl up in my lap, or make up a hopscotch board and play by myself.

He works for the Miller beer company again. He drives a cold truck and delivers beer to liquor stores and 7-Elevens. Sometimes he brings us penny candy: Bazooka bubble gum and Tootsie Rolls.

He makes good money.

"How much?" I ask.

"Enough," he says, then laughs with his head back and his mouth open and black.

"More than the president?"

"Almost."

He lives like a king.

We're not allowed to drink coffee, but Walt gives us sips of his, and sips off his beer. Our mother says, "Walt, stop that." But she laughs when she says it.

Camille has a collection of lipsticks. She's not allowed to wear them out of the house, not even to the grocery store when our mother is with us. She can't wear them into the front yard. Our mother doesn't want our neighbors to think Camille is loose.

Some of the lipsticks, half-used and broken, our mother gave Camille when she grew tired of their color. Most of them she got from restrooms in restaurants and gas stations. These are close to brand-new.

She has seven: Desert Mirage, Wine and Roses, Persuasion, Copper Penny, Hot Cocoa, Really Rose, and Pink-A-Boo.

She's not allowed to wear the Hot Cocoa; our mother says it's for black women. And she can't wear the Persuasion because it's too red and she's too young. Most times Camille wears Wine and Roses because it reminds her of the women in the movies who have a lot of cute boyfriends. Before every kiss someone yells "cut" and the actresses touch up their lipstick so they won't be forgotten. Camille says she plans to leave her mark, too. Even if she doesn't become a world-famous actress, like she wants to.

She's always looking for more, so when we finish our ice cream we tell Walt we're going to the ladies' room.

Camille picks through the garbage first. They always fall to the bottom. She pulls out the wet paper towels and hands them to me to hold and put back in the trash when she's through looking. I don't get anything for my efforts, not even a chance to try on whatever we find, but if I don't help, she kicks my ankles or punches my arm until I yell uncle and have to do it anyway.

"Jackpot!" Camille pulls out her arm. She has two lipsticks. "Evening Rose," she says. She looks at the other one and tries to push back the little sticker on the bottom. Half the fun are the names. "Damn. It's rubbed off."

When she opens it there's nothing left, not even a little stub.

"Looks like it was some kind of pink," she says. "Maybe Dreamy Pink or Peony."

We stand in front of the lipstick displays when our mother takes us to the drugstore. Camille memorizes the names. One day she'll model them in magazines.

"What's the other one look like?"

She uncaps it and rolls it all the way up. The tip is smashed but there's enough left that this is a good find. It's the kind of red — too dark — that our mother won't let Camille wear. Which is OK. Camille saves her lipsticks in a shoe box. When she's sixteen and moves away like she plans, she can wear them.

Walt is waiting outside the restroom when we come out. Camille tries to pocket our find.

"What do you have there?" he asks us.

"I found them," Camille says.

"I didn't say you didn't. What are they?" He bends closer to us, his hot breath in our faces.

"Lipstick." Camille keeps her hand closed around them. "I'm not going to use them," she says. "I just like looking at them."

"We're not allowed to wear makeup," I say. "Not out of the house. Not until we're sixteen."

"Let's see them."

"Why?" Camille has her hand with the lipsticks pushed into the front pocket of her shorts.

"A man likes lipstick just as much as you women," he says. "You know that's why you wear it, to get our attention."

"We don't wear it," I say. "We're not allowed."

"Come on." He starts us toward the door. Outside, the heat makes us sweat and makes everything white. "You can show me in the car. There's a mirror you can use to put it on.

"You can wipe it off before we get home," he says.

Camille sits in the front seat, because Walt tells her to. He pulls down the visor and opens the mirror so the light pops on; and I can see Camille's face, tight and as white as my rabbit's foot.

"Put on the lipstick, Camille," he tells her.

But she doesn't want to. Her fingers are curled around the lipstick and her knuckles are white.

"Did you hear me?" His voice is louder, and heavy. It fills up the whole car.

Camille's shoulders twitch. Her fingers open and the Evening Rose rolls onto her lap.

"You want me to help you?" Walt asks.

"No."

Camille scoots forward in her seat so she's sitting on the edge. She looks into the mirror. I can see her lips are trembling, but she moves the tip of the Evening Rose over them anyway. Twice she has to stop and use a fingertip to wipe off the extra. Walt sits behind the steering wheel, with the engine running and the air conditioner on high, while he waits for Camille to finish and show us.

"Beautiful," he says, when she's done and turns to him. "Color's perfect.

"Come here, Camille."

"No."

"You want to know what a real woman wearing lipstick feels like?" he asks.

"No."

"Yes, you do." Walt's hand snakes out and he grabs Camille by the back of her neck. He moves so he's almost on top of her and kisses her on the mouth. A long kiss. His wormy tongue licks her lips and then he moves away.

It leaves Camille's lipstick smudged. She looks like our mother does after she and Walt sit for a long time on the sofa while Camille and I are sent outside to play and we come in unexpected.

"You feel grown-up now?" he asks Camille. "You feel like a woman?"

Camille won't look in the mirror at the smudged lipstick. She wipes her hand over her mouth then uncaps the Evening Rose and runs it smoothly over her lips. She moves back to her side of the car and flips the visor up. She breathes like she's crying, like she can't get enough air.

Walt puts his arm over the seat and looks in back.

"What do you think, Chloe?" he asks me. "You ready for some lipstick?"

I think he should keep his wormy mouth to himself.

Camille is only thirteen. I tell him, "We're not allowed to wear makeup."

"What did I tell you, Camille? Your little sister needs a little more growing up."

He looks at me in the rearview mirror. "Eh, Chloe? Maybe next year you'll like lipstick?"

When Walt turns onto our street he hands Camille a napkin and she wipes off the Evening Rose.

between

I moved up the food chain. Today, I can decide between two entrees for lunch. Chicken breast or pepperoni pizza. I wait until I see them both and then make my decision. The chicken is sliced, was cooked on the grill, and is on top of a pile of lettuce. The pizza looks like it's been sitting a long time.

The oil has risen to the surface and is beginning to form like Jell-O.

"What kind of dressing?"

"What kind would her royal highness like today?"

I look over the counter. I already know it's Graciela because her English is too perfect and wrapped up in a thick Mexican accent, but her voice is so strong I don't know if she's smiling unless I see it.

"Congratulations," she says. "You're doing something right."

I haven't missed therapy once since my second month here, when I pretended to have the twenty-four-hour flu that lasted two weeks. I went down to zero in points and it took three weeks to get a bar of soap.

I've been here, at Madeline Parker, four months now. I have a brush, shampoo *and* conditioner, and library privileges.

"Thanks." Graciela is motherly. Her smile falls on me like a blanket, wraps me up, and lasts long enough I'm feeling smothered. "Do you have Ranch today?"

"For you, of course." She puts the chicken and salad on my tray, a big squirt of dressing into a plastic cup beside it, and then drops a slice of watermelon in the empty space. I stare at it for a long time, my hands sweating.

"What's wrong with you?"

"I haven't had watermelon . . ." since I sat at the kitchen table with Camille and we argued over whose lips looked more like a slice of watermelon, pink and happy.

We bought watermelon-flavored lip gloss at the drugstore that morning but had to share it. It was one of our mother's good days; she bought eye shadow for herself and later took me and Camille to the outlet stores for one dress each. The school year started weeks before, but there was no money then for clothes.

Graciela uses her plastic-covered hand to slip a second wedge of melon onto my tray.

"Now go. You're making me miss my *crios*."

I sit down at a table by myself, even though the Niña is waving at me. Girls sit in groups of two or three, leaning into the tables, talking and laughing too loud. I'm not like them. I keep to myself, but know the right words to fit in, and I use them when I need to. I am a long way from the Chloe I was meant to be, and that's what Dr. Dearborn wants me to think about. Where was I headed before my world fell apart? Before I landed somewhere in between.

There's a bus stop on the street I worked, in front of a pizza shop and not too far from the mall. There's a different kind of people on the street before dark. A lot of teenagers. They go to the mall after school and buy date dresses and eat pizza before heading home. Sometimes I think about what their homes look like.

Their yards are watered and green and the light is always on in the living room, so they know they're wanted. They have parents who call the police if they stay out too late, worried they got in a car accident. Family photos hang on the wall above the TV and cover tabletops. The kitchen smells like spaghetti, garlic, and tomatoes. I bet every girl I watched, waiting for a bus to take them back to their *castleios,* swinging plastic bags stuffed with "Kiss me" T-shirts and too-tight jeans, has her own bedroom. Posters of rock stars and pictures of the boys they love are pinned to the walls. They have a boom box and a collection of CDs they play so they can sink into another place, another time, where all their dreams come true.

I used to think like that. Before, when I had Camille and a life ahead of me. I thought I'd have a boyfriend one day, who sat on my bed after school and looked through my music collection, who picked flowers for me and held my hand. The things my father did for my mother when it was still good between them.

It feels so long ago, she seems too far away to be me. I try to hold on to that picture of her, to see what else I hoped for, what more is missing, but it grows blurry and I realize I'm about to cry. I cried a lot my first year on the street, after my stomach was full and I had a place to live. When I knew for sure there was no going back and nothing for me there anyway. And now all kinds of thoughts are swirling through my mind. What was I like? Did I want to be a doctor, an artist, a librarian? I liked school and reading. I remember that. Did I want to move to another state? Another country? Learn to speak another language? I think I might have a talent for it; I picked up the Spanish so easily.

Would I have gotten married? Had a kid?

Would I have saved my love for someone special?

These are things I will never know.

I have not held the hand of a boy.

I have not held the hand of another human being since the

day I came home from school and found Camille gone. And it was the hand of a lady police officer trying to keep me from drifting away, from looking for Camille.

On Friday nights—date night—too-blond girls pushed through the doors of the pizza shop, their boys following behind them. They chewed gum, wore shirts that showed their bellies, and said nasty things that made them laugh, and they held hands.

The girls smiled like the sun was shining.

They were happy, knowing their boys wanted them.

I don't know how to smile like that. What it would cost me to learn.

And I suppose that's who I'd be, if things were different. A girl with a boyfriend and a smile I felt on the inside.

mexican border

In our mother's old Nova, Camille and I take a pretend trip to the Mexican border. We want to buy bead necklaces and orange wrap skirts — cheap. We don't have much money, only what we managed to save from our allowance. Just across the border we can buy for half price.

We've been once, for real, when our mother and one of her boyfriends took us on a day trip. They bought statues: a wood-carved standing Jesus in prayer, and a brown mustang rearing on his hind legs. They bought the statues from the lines of vendors by the side of the freeway and wouldn't let us get out of the car.

This time we're going to mingle with the natives, Camille says. We're going to haggle for the best price.

"They're hungry for the American dollar," Camille says. "We'll talk them down to a good deal for us."

Camille is sitting on the pillows from her bed so she can see over the steering wheel. She brought her black purse that was our mother's until last year. Inside, she has her Maybelline Wine and Roses lipstick, an empty compact with a mirror she pulls out at traffic lights to check her pretend eye makeup, and a man's white handkerchief she says belonged to our father. She has no proof. But she won't use it. She keeps it pressed and folded and either in her purse or in the top drawer of her dresser, where no one, not even our mother, is allowed to go.

She also brought her favorite sweater, a green fuzzy pullover with a pearl button in the back. She brought her first bra; she has only one. And her radio.

I brought two apples from the fruit bowl on our way out of the house.

This trip is sudden. Camille found me in the backyard, in our mother's lounge chair, where I sometimes read. I have my rabbit's foot in my pocket because I don't go anywhere without it, and a dollar for the ice-cream man.

I found Simon sitting in a sun spot by the car and put him on the seat between us. He's walking on the back dash now. His claws get stuck in the stereo speakers and he has to shake them free. He makes sharp, yowling cries when this happens.

"Can't you shut that cat up?" Camille asks. "I'm trying to drive."

"His paws are stuck."

"Then unstick them," she says, and heaves a breath that messes her bangs.

By the time I reach into the backseat, Simon has taken care of it himself.

Camille drives smoothly, turning the wheel with her fingertips. She learned from watching our mother.

I'm sitting in the passenger seat. Reading the map is my responsibility, although Camille says it won't take much brain to do it.

"It's a straight shot all the way. You just look out for police," she says.

We don't want to spend all our money on a speeding ticket.

Before we get to the border it starts to rain. A squall off the ocean, Camille says. She expected it. She heard the tide warnings on the radio. "If it gets much worse, we might have to pull over."

She has the windshield wipers on high — pretend, but I can imagine them sweeping over the glass.

Camille is all scrunched up behind the wheel now. Her nose almost touches it as she leans forward and watches the pretend red taillights ahead of us. She's very good at preventing accidents.

More than once on our pretend trips she has driven off the road to avoid a bad driver. We've never flipped over or hit a tree, although we've come close.

All our trips go wrong. We never end up where we plan. Even a calm trip to the supermarket turns into a race for our lives.

"Whoever's after us wants us dead," Camille will say. She'll press harder on the gas. She'll grip the steering wheel until her knuckles are white. And she'll shout orders at me, "Duck!" Or, if her attention is needed somewhere else, "Grab the wheel!" This, when she pretend-shoots at the car behind us.

This trip is no different.

"Will you look at that," Camille says. "We're being followed."

"Where?"

"Don't turn around! Idiot! We don't want him to know we know," she hisses.

"It's that green Chevy, with the Nevada license plates. He's been with us the last ten miles. Every time I make a lane change, he changes, too.

"Damn rain," she mutters. She turns on the high beams. "We might have to get off."

Every time, there's a reason to get off the freeway. Sometimes the sky's a dark Satan. Sometimes there's a moon. Today, Camille says, the thunderclouds will make it hard to see two feet in front of us.

Sometimes the other car will turn off its lights and coast behind us while we drive down a dead-end street.

We should keep going, I tell her. Stay on the road until we see a gas station.

Sometimes Camille will bring up the possibility of a gas station. If we could only find a gas station, she'll say, only to find it deserted when we pull into it. Not even the bell rings.

"Who's scared now?" Camille says.

"I'm not scared."

"Yes, you are."

"Not as scared as you. I won't cry."

This morning Camille cried. She locked herself in our bedroom and told me to leave her alone. She played the radio, singing over Britney Spears. She had it up really loud and still I heard only her voice.

Walt got her for eating the last bit of Cheerios for breakfast. That's what set him off, but really it was because last night Camille bit him. She kicked his shins and yelled to wake the dead. When our mother stumbled into our bedroom, Walt told her Camille had a nightmare.

This morning he chased her around the kitchen and out the front door. Mrs. Pitts was in her front yard clipping the wisteria bush.

"I hate Mrs. Pitts," Camille said. I hate her, too.

All our high-speed chases, every shoot-out and game of chicken turn out the same. The man after us is wearing a ski mask or a Halloween costume. We can't see his face, not until the end, after we've killed him and Camille takes off his mask to reveal his identity. He's either slumped over the wheel in the driver's seat and Camille has to use all her strength to push him back so she can peel off his ski cap and see who he is. Or he's thrown clear of the car and lies mangled, arms and legs everywhere, according to Camille, and she rolls him over and takes off his mask and there he is: an old boyfriend of our mother's.

We get out of the car and walk over to where the body was thrown clear.

"Look at that," Camille says. "His arm is missing." She scans the driveway. "You see it anywhere?"

"No."

I let Simon out with us. I watch him walk through the grass toward the Portsmiths' backyard.

Camille crouches down beside the body and takes a long time straightening his head. "A clown's mask," she says, then peels it off.

It's Walt.

"He's a dirty SOB," Camille says. "I don't like him."

She rubs her palms like she's trying to clean them under water.

"Now we can get our skirts," I say.

I really want an orange wrap skirt and a string of different-color beads that tell the future. I want to keep pretending. To see how far Camille will go. Lately, our trips end after she lets her hate loose.

"I don't care about the skirts," Camille says.

"I do."

"Then drive yourself."

"I don't know how to drive."

She walks away and I see the backs of her legs just below the hem of her yellow sundress. Purple and blue hand marks where Walt got her.

"You need to learn. I'll show you."

Camille gets Simon from where he's sitting on the edge of the Portsmiths' yard, then gets in on the passenger side. She puts Simon on her lap and keeps him there by holding onto his scruff. He stretches his back and purrs as she pets him.

"Put the key in the ignition." She pretends to put the car in neutral. "Now, start and we're off."

I make sure to steer clear of the place where we left Walt. Camille likes to run her victims over. She does this whooping like a warrior Indian.

Now she's crying. I tell her she's going to ruin her makeup. She's always careful about that. She doesn't want to look like our mother looks when she cries, like she has two black eyes.

She pulls our father's handkerchief from her purse and wipes her face.

"It doesn't smell like him anymore," she says.

fire-eater

The little Niña is going home. She's no longer a harm to herself.

In group the doctors ask her about the time she jumped out her bedroom window and she says, That was a mistake. I'll never do that again.

When they ask her, Can we trust you with an open medicine cabinet? With knives in plain view?

She says, I'm not thinking about dying. I have a job to do. I have a future.

She once put her hand into an open flame on the gas stove in her kitchen. She kept it there for a count of ten.

What about causing yourself unnecessary pain? they ask.

Can they trust her not to burn her arms with cigarettes?

Will she promise to eat three meals a day?

Will she look before crossing the street? Think before opening a bottle of aspirin?

She once ate fire.

She made a funnel with construction paper, soaked it with gasoline, and lit a match to it. Then she took a breath, in and out, quick.

Will she be doing this again?

No, she tells them. I'm past that. My mind is on other things. I want to make the world a better place to live in.

No pain . . . no pain . . . no pain . . .

Don't feel . . . don't feel . . . don't feel . . .

That's how she did it, put her hand in the flame from the kitchen stove and counted to ten and survived with nothing to show for it. No scars. No souvenirs.

"I listen to the words. I believe that what I'm saying is true: I feel no pain.

"Then I do it. I do it while the words are everything.

"If you don't fear it, you're OK. Nothing happens. But think about it, and you're lost."

Her hand never burned, she says. It was sore for a while. She put some Bactine on it and it was OK. Like a sunburn. But there were no blisters. No scarring. And she's telling the truth. She holds out her hands for me to see. There are no marks of old wounds or punishments.

No one would even know about it, except her mother caught her in the act. She came into the kitchen and saw the Niña with her hand in the open flame and she screamed to bring down the house. Then she called 911, not even thinking to get the Niña away from the stove.

"It wouldn't have been sore," she tells me, "except she interrupted my thoughts. I lost my focus."

It's all in the head, she says.

There are promises the Niña must make before they'll let her go. She'll sign a contract. We all will. There's no leaving unless we agree to come back, once a week for as long as it takes. We'll get a real job. Pee in a cup. And no calling people from the past, they're more weight than we can bear.

We leave knowing we'll be fighters the rest of our lives. *Guerreras.* Our problems can come back, if we let them. If we're not careful. Vigilant. So we can leave Madeline Parker, but on a leash.

The Niña will sign her contract just to get out. She'll sign it so she can get on with her life. She's tired of living in limbo. Of feeling like a ropewalker without a net.

Just about everyone expects us to fall. And when we do, it's up to us alone to scrape it all back together.

"My life is set," she says.

They have her organized. A half day of school until she feels better. One hour a week with her private therapist and an hour in group here at Madeline Parker. She'll have family therapy with her mother. She'll have chores to do around the house. After-school activities will have to wait. Maybe a part-time job in the summer.

We say good-bye to the Niña the night before she goes. We have a little party, with cake and music and staff telling her why they think she'll do OK out there, why they don't expect to see her back here anytime soon.

"Your life has new meaning," they say. "You understand your mother and she understands you."

In the morning the Niña packs her bags. She packs everything except her diary.

"I want you to have it," she says. "We're a lot alike."

I don't think so and I tell her this.

"But we are." She says we're both where we're at in life because of a brother or a sister. "And our mothers are just the same." She knows this because things never should have gone so far.

I start wishing I never said anything about Camille or about our mother's boyfriends. That I'd never showed them what growing up Chloe was like. And besides, she's wrong. It's not Camille who got me where I am today. Not the way the Niña's brother did her.

And one more thing, she says. "We changed our names thinking it'd change who we are." Thinking we could have a different life.

Her doctor told her that.

"We're running away." With nowhere to go.

Dr. Dearborn has been after me to come up with a new last name. One that says I'm somebody. He thinks I chose Doe to make a statement. One that didn't require an explanation. A statement I no longer need because my life is changing. I have a future.

The Niña leaves the diary on her bed. She says we're almost sisters. I think about that. Could we be sisters? Not the way Camille and I were, but because our lives are too much alike, the markings on our bodies too much the same, this could be our bond. She could be my little sister, and maybe having one wouldn't be so bad.

I don't tell her I'll think about it, but I will.

espanto

D r. Dearborn says there's a moment when someone like me knows they've come to the end of the line. When did I decide I couldn't do it anymore? When did I decide to leave the only home I knew? Could I tell him about that moment?

I've been in Madeline Parker five months now; I've lost

track of how many times I sat in this little room, just me and my *doctor,* how many sins I've confessed.

"I lived a long time wishing I could leave my mother's house." I shrug. "I had nowhere to go."

"When did that stop mattering?" he asks.

When was nowhere better than where I was?

"I found Camille. In the backyard."

We'd only been back to school a month and Walt had come to our bedroom door and told Camille, No, not today. He'd started doing that toward the end, kept Camille home from school. Every time he did, Camille cried, but not that morning.

The first thing I did when I got home was look for her. She hated our house and our bedroom and I always found her outside, sometimes crying, sometimes so still she was almost invisible, sitting in the yard with Simon or with a bunch of flowers she'd gathered and plucked, holding the soft petals in her hands like she was trying to capture water.

"She was laying down." At first, from a distance, I thought she looked like a white, white sheet that had been blown from a clothesline. "When I got close I knew why.

"I screamed. And kept screaming."

"What was wrong with Camille?"

I ignore his question. I don't want to say it. I'm not ready to say it. And, anyway, he already knows.

"Mrs. Pitts called the police."

They came with an ambulance.

A fire truck. Two.

They came in pairs.

In cars with lights swirling and sirens splitting the air.

The *policía,* with their guns and badges and vests like they were walking into a war zone, came too late.

They said, Why don't you come over here? Come with me. Come into the house.

"They made me sit on the couch. I was still holding Camille's shoes and they took them from me."

The police asked, Do you know where your mother is?

My mother was working.

"Do you have her phone number? At work? Do you know your mother's telephone number?"

I stop. My chest feels tight. I don't think I can go on.

"I can't talk now," I tell him.

I'm a dam about to burst.

"You're doing fine," he says. He leans forward, rests his elbows on his knees. It's his all-star pose, if he was ever a player.

"You like bringing me to tears?"

"It's my job," the doctor says. "I want you to go farther today. I want you to give me a little more."

He says, "Tell me what you were feeling." On that day. "On September nineteenth."

Like a knife was stuck in my ribs and everytime I drew a breath my lungs burned. Like I was dying from the inside out.

"Do you know the word *espanto?*"

No. He doesn't know any Spanish.

"And you're living in the City of Angels?"

He's not a native. He moved here from Wisconsin to go to UCLA. He looks OK today.

"Did your wife dress you?"

"Yes," he says. "She went shopping over the weekend. Do you like it?" He pulls on the collar of his new blue cotton shirt with the gray pearl buttons.

"You look like you're playing dress-up cowboy." But it's good. "It's better."

"Can you order a taco in Spanish? Ask for directions? Call for help?"

He says maybe he can order off a menu in Spanish.

"Well, in case you ever need it, it's *ayuda!* If you're ever away from home. If you venture into the *barrios*." But the slums are no place for an innocent.

He takes off his glasses and his eyes look smaller today, deeper.

"You were afraid," he says. On that day.

He wants me to say it, to own my feelings, and we've come too far for me to deny him. For me to hide.

"*Espanto*, it means terror." My voice breaks just a little and a smile fills the lines in his face. It hits me like a sucker punch.

"Good," he says.

"You want me scared?"

"Anything else would be a lie."

I know he's right, but I don't like it. I sit real still for a minute, and think about how it feels. To be afraid. It turns the edges of my world white. Makes my heart beat too fast. My lungs burn. My eyes, too.

"Don't stop now," he says. We're close. My breakthrough, he can see it just around the corner. So can I. I have to work harder to breathe, like I'm standing at the top of Everest, and I'm light-headed.

"Isn't that enough?" I can't make my voice more than a whisper.

But he shakes his head. There'll be no rest for me. Not until I give it all I've got.

I take a minute. Until my hands stop shaking and I can look him in the eye.

"The police didn't take him. Not right away."

Walt walked around the house with a gun. For three days. He balanced it on his leg when he watched TV and set it beside his plate when he ate. That morning, the morning they arrested Walt, he held it to his head, above his ear, and asked us,

"How does that look? You want this to be the last picture you have of me?" We didn't answer. "Chloe, get the camera."

I took the picture, with him looking straight at me, with the gun against his head and his finger curled around the trigger.

He asked my mother, "Well, how does it look? You want me to do it, don't you?"

My mother said, "Why don't you do it? Instead of talking about it?" She got up from the table, where only Walt was eating, where I was sitting with a glass of orange juice, and she stabbed the air with her cigarette. I wished it was his heart she was slicing into. I wished the gun would go off on its own.

"Because I knew he wouldn't do it, Doc. He was a coward."

Walt said, "You don't love me anymore? You don't love me, Connie?"

My mother looked at him. Her eyes seemed deeper than the ocean. She took a drag off the cigarette, but her hand was shaking.

"You know it was an accident. I didn't mean it to happen. You know how she got me going all the time." His hand tightened on the gun. He pushed it against his head. "Is this what you want, then? Answer me, Connie. You better answer me. Because if you don't love me anymore, I want to be dead."

I finally tell Dr. Dearborn what he's been waiting for: "He killed my sister. And my mother knew it."

The room started spinning. I held on to the edge of the table, felt my fingertips slipping.

I remember thinking, Don't answer him. Don't answer him. I tried to think it hard enough that I could make her stay quiet. If she could do it, if she could let him think she didn't love him anymore, even if she did, there would be a chance for us. I wouldn't have to leave like I was already thinking I'd do. We could move again, like we did when Henrik left, when my father left, and start over. I wasn't ready to give up on my mother yet.

But the meanness drained out of Walt. He was like a puppy pushing at her hand, looking for love.

"Oh, God," she said. "Oh, God, help me." She was crying again; her face folded up and her cigarette fell from her fingers. "Oh, God. Oh, God. Oh, God!"

"Are you still my wife, Connie?" Walt put a little whine in his voice, a little uncertainty. "Are we together?" His hand, holding the gun to his head, shook. "I don't want to be here if we're not together."

"I'm your wife."

She said the words softly, like they cost her nothing. But her face changed. She was an old woman with white in her red hair and a wrinkled face.

"It was over then," I tell the doctor. "For all of us.

"Camille was dead and I felt that way too."

Only I was still breathing. I tried to make myself stop, thought if I wished it hard enough, it'd happen.

And that's how I was feeling. Like a *muñón*. A ghost. I was what was left over after the best part of me was taken away. And I kept thinking it couldn't be true. Like the people who lose an arm, who still have feeling in their missing fingers. I could still feel Camille.

The police came back three days after Camille was killed because what they took out of her was semen. They came to the door and said,

"Mr. Atwater, could you step outside for a minute? There are some questions . . . a few things that need clearing up."

"Why don't you come in?"

"Outside would be better. There's no need to upset the girl."

I was standing at the door, next to Walt. Inside my head I was screaming his name, but I couldn't find my voice. I was still in that faraway place I went when I first found Camille, where it felt like I wasn't really living all the things that were happening.

Walt was waiting for the police. He had the .357 in his jeans, under his San Diego Zoo T-shirt. He pulled out the gun and said he would kill himself. He put it to his head and told them not to come near him. To stay away, or he'd do it. Sure as they were looking at him alive, they'd be looking at him dead.

My mother flew out of the house to be at Walt's side. To try to get him to put the gun down.

"No, Walt. No! You don't mean it." Her face was swollen and pink, from days of crying. "You don't mean it. Tell me you don't mean it."

She cradled his head in her hands. Looked into his eyes. Stuck her body up against his. Clung to him like she wouldn't be parted.

"I want to die. You know I want to die."

I wanted him to die, too. I wanted it more than I wanted to breathe.

The police swarmed around them. They took the gun and tore my mother out of Walt's arms and held her back. They pushed Walt down on top of the car and pulled his arms back and Walt was crying, "I love you! I love you, Connie! You know I love you!"

Even after they shut the door, he pushed his face up against the glass so his nose and lips were smashed, and he said, "Connie! Connie!" Like a baby bawling. "Connie!"

And that was the last I saw of him. This man who killed my sister.

"And your mother? When did you last see her?"

I take a deep breath but it's not enough.

"Your wife buy you anything else? Maybe some shoes?"

"When, Chloe?"

"Some *zapatos*. Loafers or Nikes. Do you run?"

"Your mother."

"Your mother, Doc."

He almost laughs.

"I'm not letting you off," he says. "It's my last question today. When you answer it you can go back to your room."

"Or we'll sit here till Tuesday?"

"For as long as it takes."

But I'm done hiding.

"Six years ago September twenty-second," I tell him. "Three days after Camille was killed." I stand up and move toward the door. "It rained, for the first time since before summer. It was hard to breathe, with the steam coming up off the pavement." I get to the door and turn the knob.

"I left that night, when my mother came back from the police station. It was dark. The street lights were on. She came into the house and sat down at the kitchen table, her purse in her lap, and I asked her, 'What are we going to do?'

"She couldn't look at me. She just sat there for a long time, and then she said, 'He's my husband.'

"I was on the street two months when the police picked me up. The first time. They put me in a foster home. That's no place for a child."

I step through the door but look back at him.

"I took one thing with me. You know what that was?"

He shakes his head.

"A picture of my father. The only one we had. I kept it with me two years. Then it was just one more thing to carry around."

He nods, like he understands. And maybe he does. I know I'm not the only person who's had to give up a dream.

I shut the door. I think he's probably right about talking, that bad memories lose their hold on you once they hit air.

monkey ring

"Camille was wearing a yellow headband, a plastic monkey ring she got out of the gum-ball machine at Safeway, and a Band-Aid on the heel of her right foot, where her new school shoes dug into her."

It took a whole week for her to break the shoes in. She

limped like something was broken, and she thought she might need crutches if it kept up.

"You remember a lot about that day," Dr. Dearborn says.

"I remember the things that were important to Camille."

"Good. That's how we keep loved ones close." No matter the distance.

No matter how they were taken from you.

"Tell me about that day," he says. "Your last day with your sister."

The police asked Walt, "You were at work?"

He was wearing his work shirt that said *Miller Genuine Draft* above the pocket. The police asked Walt how long he was a driver for Miller.

"Eight years."

"Are you fond of the daughters?"

Walt shoved his hands in his pockets. He rocked on the heels of his feet. "I love them," he said. "Camille was a good girl."

The police stopped writing and studied Walt.

"Yeah? So when I call Miller they'll tell me you were on the job?"

"That's what they'll say."

"And your last delivery was where?"

"Well, I don't remember," Walt said. "I guess I forgot now. I forgot."

"Yeah, well, it's written down, right?"

"I don't write down all my drops. Some are called in at the last minute."

"Then Miller will know about it? The guy who radioed you out?"

"He must know. Someone has to keep track of us."

I found her in the backyard and covered her with rose petals and the oak leaves that turned gold in the Indian summer.

The police asked, "Did you find her like that already? Or did you use the petals and the leaves to cover her up?"

"She was naked."

"So you wanted to cover her up?"

I shrugged and it was enough for him.

"Did you do anything else?" the cop asked, leaning forward, leaning into my breath. "Did you maybe close her eyes?"

He used his sky blue handkerchief to wipe my face. "Do you think that might have happened?"

"I thought maybe she could be asleep. I wanted her to be asleep."

But she wasn't.

The police called my mother at work and told her to come home. I heard them tell her, "It's about Camille. Why don't you come home right away." But when she got there, Camille was gone. The ambulance left with her on a stretcher; they put plastic bags over her hands and taped her mouth shut. I watched from the upstairs window.

"What is it? What is it?" my mother asked.

The police lady was trying to tell her. She was bending over my mother, who was sitting next to Walt on the plastic chairs we bought to sun ourselves. She talked softly, but I heard her through the glass. "I'm sorry. I'm really sorry. Camille was killed today. This afternoon . . . Camille was killed."

And my mother kept saying "What is it? What is it?" like she couldn't hear anything, not even her own voice, because it got louder and louder until it blended with the sirens, until it sounded like a whistle.

"What kind of relationship does Mr. Atwater have with your children?"

"He doesn't like kids," my mother explained. "He yelled at them from time to time. It's just because he doesn't like kids."

"Were your children safe with Mr. Atwater?"

"What do you mean?"

"Did you ever leave them with Mr. Atwater, maybe when you went to the grocery store?"

"Yes. A lot of times. He just didn't want them underfoot. They had to stay in their room or outside."

"He ever hit them?"

"No. Never."

"Chloe says he spanked them."

"Well, yes. But not hit them. He never hit them. Sometimes he'd whop them on their behind if they were acting up. That's all."

"Aren't they too old for spanking?"

"He didn't spank them, really. He'd just whop them once or twice on the behind."

"But you'd leave them for an hour or two and come back and everything was fine?"

"Yes."

"Camille had burns on her hands. Do you know how that happened?"

"Her curling iron?" My mother had her hands in her shirt, twisting. "I don't know. Was it her curling iron?"

"No, ma'am. They don't look like burns from a curling iron. These burns look more like they came from a cigarette." The policeman sat down in front of my mother, on the vinyl footrest. "Do you smoke, ma'am?"

My mother's hands grew still. "Yes, I smoke. I smoke. Why? You don't think I burned her? I didn't burn her."

"Who did, ma'am?'

My mother began to thread her hands through her hair. I watched the red strands sift through her fingers, then she pulled at the ends, pulled like she meant to tear her hair out. "I don't know."

"I think you do. You understand Camille isn't coming back."

"I know! I know that. I know."

"Somebody did those burns."

"I don't know who. It wasn't Walt. I know you're thinking Walt. You're thinking Walt, but he didn't do it."

"But Mr. Atwater smokes, doesn't he, ma'am?"

"Did you ask him?"

"Does he smoke, ma'am?"

"Yes."

She was bent over and holding her stomach with her hands. Her beautiful eyes, like none we'd ever seen, were sinking in her swollen face.

train

The little Niña returns for group therapy once a week. She sits in a circle with us other contessas still waiting to get out and shares her life in the land of the free. Her brother, it turns out, is never coming home.

"He's dead," she tells us. "He's gone."

She doesn't say whether she misses him. Whether she thinks now she'll be able to live a normal life, not waiting for him to come back and pick up where he left off.

"We buried him at Green Hills Cemetery." They have a family plot. "They killed him." The other boys who couldn't live with a saint among them. With a white boy walking around calling himself *Hey-Zeus*. "There are gangs in prison."

The doctor asks, "Do you feel safe, Tammy?"

"I feel like he knows everything I'm doing. Just like God."

Next group, the Niña doesn't show. The banana-yellow Lexus doesn't pull up the circular drive and drop her at the door, no little Niña walking without looking back, even when her mother calls,

"Tammy! Tammy, have a good session!"

She was determined to leave her mother behind.

This time the Niña was successful.

The newspaper said *Girl, 14, Throws Herself at Train*. But that wasn't the way it happened. They think it must have been a split-second decision. That she couldn't have waited. She couldn't have thought it out and then waited patiently for the end of her life. It was unthinkable. It made a person cringe. It made them stop a beat or two. It's easier for those who've never been there to think the Niña had a moment when the world piled itself on her shoulders all at once — we all have those moments — and she was in the wrong place at the wrong time. If she was anywhere else, the mall, for example, she'd be with us today.

But it's not true.

Some of the girls here say, She was desperate for love. She was some kind of Juliet. It was missing that brother of hers and finding a way they could be together.

That's not true either. Later, after the staff sat us down and told us about it, after we read about it in the newspaper, I took out her diary and read about it there.

She'd practiced. She'd rehearsed her death and then wrote about it in her diary. She thought it would happen so quickly, the speed of the train would fling her body into the sky, arms and legs wide, her mouth an open and screeching *No* and she would stay there, caught forever at the moment of impact and hanging over the world like a star. In the margins of her diary she drew a picture of herself exactly like that, with smaller stars blinking around her.

She wanted to get it right, so she'd tried it, right before they locked her up in Madeline Parker: She'd laid herself down on the railroad tracks near Busman Street and waited for the Georgia–Pacific. She'd felt the ties vibrate like it was an earthquake, long before she saw the train round the curve and bear down on her.

She'd had a full two minutes to think about what she was doing before the nose of the train was pointed in her direction. Its thunderous clacking on the rails beat over her. It'd made it so she could think of very little. It'd filled her head, so nothing else could. Hypnotized her so she almost lost the will to lift herself off the tracks and throw herself into the gravel and sage weed. And when it passed, it'd been like she was in the center of a hurricane. She'd been caught in a vacuum. She'd held to a large rock, feeling her fingers slip, the skin shaving off. She knew she wouldn't feel a thing.

This time, she meant it for keeps, and she left a piece of paper behind, the curling end of a piece of paper towel, stuffed into the front pocket of her jeans. She'd written her name on it. Her real name. This I got from the newspaper, along with the fact that the Niña had died instantly.

She knew who she was and couldn't live with it.

The doctors ask, "What other options did Tammy have?"

I think everything she tried to hold on to slipped through her fingers. Including her life.

I know now that the little Niña was right about one thing: She and I were a lot alike. Our mothers failed us. Our bodies were not our own. Our names were not the ones we were born to. And we gave up. Even though suicide wasn't my way, living on the streets and using my body was like dying, a quiet death no one really noticed.

But there's still time for me to change my mind. And I'm thinking that's exactly what I want to do. Live.

I decide it's time to come up with a new name. I can never go back to who I was before I lost Camille. Before Walt came into our lives. Before our mother drifted away from us. I'll never be that girl again. But I can do better than Doe. Tammy was right to leave her diary with me. Reading it, I felt like I was looking at myself in places. I felt some of the same things she felt. And reading her death exactly like she planned it, knowing what she was feeling, set me free in a way. I swear I heard glass shattering. It was like breaking through the water and taking my first real breath. It burned my lungs going down. Made me realize I was still alive. That I want to go on feeling that way.

I tell the doctors, "Tammy did all she could for herself." She was beyond the touch of our hands, the sound of our voices.

But I'm not. I'm right here.

hoot owl

The first thing he asks me this session:

"Have you decided on a last name?"

Ever since I told him I was thinking about it, he's made it his mission to see it done. For three weeks I've been writing letters out on a piece of paper and trying to make them fit and mean something. I sit on my bed and look at the empty bed beside me, where the Niña once sat staring at old photographs. Where she'd left her diary, hoping I'd read it. I'm glad I did. I know now how easily it could have been me.

Today he tells me I'll need a real name for my Social Security card. For my paycheck. A bank account. To rent a real apartment. For all the things I'll need in the land of the living.

I tell him I have it.

He waits with his eyes wide open behind his glasses. He looks like an owl. I tell him so and he says he's ready to start hooting.

"You always been a cheerleader?"

He says he first noticed his optimism in college. "I wasn't big enough to play ball," he admits. So the next best thing was to cheer them on.

"You feel that way about me, Doc? Your life wasn't messed up enough to put you on the street so now you spend your time with girls like me?"

"Don't think there isn't someone out there waiting for your help," he says.

"As bad as my life was, there's always someone worse off?"

"No," he says. "No matter how bad it gets, we always have something worth giving."

"You went to church on Sunday."

He doesn't deny it.

"I used to see things that way. Life is a bowl of cherries."

"No reason you can't think that way again." But he doesn't push it. "Your name?"

I have a list, but what I really want is to take some part of Camille with me. I tell him this.

"How will you do that?"

I knew he'd ask. I realize now he didn't solve my problems; he gave me what I needed to solve them myself.

"I used the letters of her name."

He likes my strategy.

"I chose the one that showed I was going somewhere."

This makes him even happier. He sits back in his chair, smiling.

"Aimes."

"Chloe Aimes. I like that."

So do I.

courage

There are milestones. The first month, eighty percent of us return to the old life. If we make it six months, we have a fighting chance. One year and we're as cured as we're going to be. Twenty, thirty years later, gray and slow, there's a chance we'll return. Like alcoholics, we'll live with it every day. That's what they say, but on my year anniversary I don't feel any pull. That life seems like someone else's.

"Because you stayed in therapy," the doctor says. I never gave up on him. Or myself.

Every Tuesday I leave my job at the Vets Administration, where I greet patients and schedule follow-up appointments, a little early. I hop on the 19 and return to the old homestead for ninety minutes in that tiny room with no air. Except they cut him a window.

"Are you happy with that?" I ask him.

"It's getting better." He smiles like he's a winner. "By next year I'll have an air conditioner."

Perseverance. It's his favorite word. We've spent more than one session defining it.

It's a guarantee.

You'll get what you want, eventually.

Athletes know it as endurance.

Politicians call it patience.

CEOs have ambition.

Actors have devotion.

I have courage.

The End.